Dear Readers,

The last rose of summer may be fading, but Bouquet romances bloom all year long! And for this back-to-school month—which often means more reading time for Mom—we've got four delightful, heart-warming stories to enhance those late-summer afternoons in the hammock, the porch swing, or even the rocking chair.

After 25 Harlequin novels, it's high time for Vanessa Grant to grace Zebra with **If You Loved Me.** When Emma's 18-year-old son goes missing on a kayaking trip in the Northwest wilderness, Emma has no choice but to put herself at the mercy of onetime lover Gary McKenzie—an outdoorsman with his own plane. He knows every inch of the territory—but can he find his way back into Emma's heart?

It's a long way from high society Boston to Little Fork, Wyoming, but Caitlyn makes the trip when she inherits half a ranch, never dreaming that a sinfully handsome partner will be part of the deal. And who would have dreamed that **Caitlyn's Cowboy** would melt the ice around her heart? Gina Jackson makes her Bouquet debut with this captivating tale of magical love.

Newcomer Susan Hardy sweeps her readers into the breathtaking North Carolina mountains, where free-spirited Clementine "Clem" Harper is reluctantly swept into the arms of city slicker Will Fletcher. Will soon discovers that it's not easy to win the heart of a mountain gal . . . until he learns the secrets of **Mountain Magic.**

Veteran romance writer Judy Gill's **All in the Family** features two meddling daughters who can't resist "fixing-up" newly divorced Dad Jett Cotts with one of their teachers. Karen Anderson is reluctant at first, but somehow this handsome, athletic, warmhearted man makes her feel cherished for the first time in ages. Maybe matchmaking isn't such a bad idea after all!

Kick back, slip off your shoes, and settle down for a nice, long read. Let your eyes follow your heart into these four enthralling romances . . . and before you know it, it will be next month—and time for four more. Enjoy!

The Editors

CHAMPAGNE AND KISSES

After another dance and a last glass of champagne, they left the restaurant.

Will noticed that Clem was peering straight up at the sky. "What is it?" he asked, following her gaze. "Does champagne make you see flying saucers?"

Clem didn't laugh at his joke. "I can't see the stars," she said, and he could hear the sadness in her voice. "The city lights are too bright."

"Come with me," Will said. "I'll show you something that's just as good as the stars."

Upstairs in his apartment, Clem felt the tension creeping into her chest. Would he kiss her?

Will pulled aside the heavy drapes that covered the outer wall . . . a wall of glass. Clem looked out onto Manhattan at midnight. It was breathtaking. Central Park sprawled beneath them. Beyond it were the skyscrapers, lit up in all their glory.

"It's magnificent," she said.

He put his arms around her and drew her closer to him. "Not nearly as magnificent as you," he whispered. He brought his lips down on hers—gently at first, then with more urgency.

He would use the next week, he promised himself, to make her fall in love with him—and with New York. And when the time was right, she'd be his. She'd stay. Maybe . . .

MOUNTAIN MAGIC

SUSAN HARDY

Zebra Books
Kensington Publishing Corp.

http://www.zebrabooks.com

ZEBRA BOOKS are published by

Kensington Publishing Corp.
850 Third Avenue
New York, NY 10022

First Printing: September, 1999
10 9 8 7 6 5 4 3 2 1

Printed in the United States of America

ONE

"A sapphire!" Clementine's shout echoed down the valley from the bank of the mountain stream. She put the stone to her lips, moistened it, and scrubbed her finger across the top to reveal the rich, lustrous color.

She sat down on the bank to examine her prize more carefully, quickly judging the potential of the stone with her trained eye. It would become a cabochon pendant, she thought, set in silver. She drew in her breath as the stone caught a glint of sunlight and glowed as if lit by a fire within.

"Ruby? Where are you, dog? I just found a keeper! It's not the rock that'll save Uncle Jess's shop, but it's . . . Ruby?"

Clementine heard a familiar jingling sound, but not in time to avoid a blow from behind from a large bundle of fur and energy. The impact caused the stone to fly out of her grasp and land in the stream with a loud plop.

"Ruby! Look what you've done! Can't you learn to put on the brakes a little sooner?"

At the scolding, the half-grown golden retriever lumbered two steps back, sat down, and hung her head. Twisting her muzzle to one side, she gave Clementine a look so sheepish and contrite that her mistress had to laugh.

"Oh, all right. You're forgiven." She hugged the dog, causing Ruby to raise a small cloud of dust with her wagging tail. "The least you can do is help me find that stone again."

Clementine got down on all fours next to the place in the stream where she thought she'd lost the rock. Ruby, thinking this was a new game, splashed into the stream, getting herself and the red bandanna she wore around her neck thoroughly soaked.

"You're a big help," Clem muttered. "All you're doing is muddying the water so I can't see a thing." She reached into the stream and brought out two handfuls of rocks and mud, which she spread out on the bank. When she was sure the missing sapphire was not among the first batch, she turned back to the stream to continue her dredging.

William Bartholomew Fletcher III sat on the fallen log beside the hiking trail and reached for his canteen. As he took a drink, he looked out over the mountains around and below him. Even though it had been years since he'd taken a real vacation, he hadn't realized how much he'd needed one until now. He'd only arrived in North Carolina the day before, but he already felt revitalized. He was sure that a week or two of rest and relaxation would cure his minor case of burnout. *Well, not really burnout,* he thought. It wasn't like he was about to lose his edge or anything.

Edge, he thought wryly—when applied to him, some people called it killer instinct. Call it what you would, without "it" on Wall Street, you were nobody.

And he was definitely somebody in the financial world—the top man in New York's most prestigious investment firm. One of the most influential men on "the Street."

His picture frequently appeared in the pages of *Forbes*. His name was often dropped by *Wall Street Journal* financial writers. From corporate raiding to arranging multimillion dollar deals selling chunks of Manhattan real estate to the Japanese, he'd done it all.

Maybe that's my problem, he mused. *Maybe all I need is a new challenge.* He didn't know what it was, but something was definitely missing from his life. It wasn't that he didn't enjoy his work—in fact, he thrived on it—but there was some small part of him that was empty, unsatisfied. Maybe this vacation would give him some insights into what he needed.

As he rose and started back up the trail, he heard a noise that sounded like a cry, and a feminine one at that. Maybe someone needed help. He set off in the direction of the shout.

Having gone through another batch of rocks without success, Clementine was exasperated. Sitting back on her heels, she clasped her hands together and squeezed her eyes tightly shut. "Oh, please, let me find what I'm looking for. Let me find what I need more than anything else." She sighed deeply and reached halfway up to her elbows in the stream.

Ruby let out a shrill bark. Startled by the dog's sudden outburst, Clementine jumped, lost her balance, and fell face-first into the stream. She rolled over onto her side and sat up, sputtering, to face a very amused-looking man.

"You know," the stranger said, smirking, "if I were you I'd pick a deeper body of water for diving practice. You could wind up with a nasty headache that way."

Sitting waist-deep in the stream, Clementine looked up at the tall, dark, *handsome* stranger. About six feet tall and with a muscular build, he had thick, unruly black hair and truly startling blue eyes. He wore an expensive-looking outfit—khaki shorts and shirt, boots that looked hardly worn, a backpack—and a smile that crinkled the corners of his eyes and mouth in a way that caused Clementine's breath to catch in her throat. The rock was momentarily forgotten.

Ruby issued a throaty but half-hearted growl as Clementine continued to size up the stranger.

"Do you speak, too, or do you let your dog do all the talking?" The man took a few steps closer, bent down, and extended his hand. She took it, and he hauled her from the water with ease.

His hand clasping hers, Will looked into the face of the young woman. She was half covered with mud and her wet hair hung about her face in clumps. Looking her up and down, he decided that despite the mud her oval face was strikingly pretty. She blinked water droplets away from eyes as green as their forest surroundings. The way her wet clothing clung to her tall, willowy frame warmed his blood.

"Well?" he asked.

Clementine began to cough. Until she tried to speak, she hadn't realized she'd inhaled a gulp of water. The man let go of her hand and patted her back gently.

"Who are you?" she finally gasped.

"I'm Will Fletcher. I was hiking up the trail and I

heard a noise, so I decided to come over and investigate. I thought someone might need help. Now it looks as if I've done more harm than good. I almost caused you to drown in a foot of water."

Ruby let out a friendly "woof" and resumed wagging her tail, having decided that the stranger was not a threat.

"Nice dog. I love golden retrievers," Will said, bending down to give Ruby's head a scratch. Turning back to Clem, he said, "And you are—?"

"Clementine Harper. Clem, to my friends."

"Well, I certainly hope we can be friends." Will fixed her with a disarming smile.

Oh, you do, do you? Clem thought. It wasn't unusual to run into other rock hunters or hikers in these woods. She guessed she should be wary, being alone with a strange man. Her instincts told her he was all right, though. Well, more than all right, actually. In fact, her breathing hadn't quite returned to its normal rhythm, and she suspected it had nothing to do with fright.

"Well, friend, how about a favor?" Clem said, wiping some of the mud from her forearms. "You could help me find the rock I just lost in the stream." She pointed to the expensive hiking boots and grinned. "That is, if you aren't afraid of getting those brand new boots dirty."

Will laughed. "That sounds like a dare. Sure, I'll help. What are we looking for?"

Clem picked up a twig, squatted down, and drew a geometric pattern in the dirt. Will let the backpack slide off his arms and set it aside. He squatted down across from Clem's drawing.

"Looks like a chevron," he observed.

"That's right. These overlapping triangles form

the crystal structure of corundum found in this area. So we're looking for a rock with that shape." Clem searched his face for any understanding of the significance of her explanation, and saw none. "Oh, yes, and it's pink."

"Corundum. Great," Will said, petting Ruby, who had interpreted his crouching down to her level as an invitation for a big, wet kiss on the cheek. "What's corundum?" he asked as Ruby licked his face.

Clem laughed. "You're not from around here, are you?" Everyone in the state of North Carolina knew this was sapphire and ruby country. All you had to do was drive around and see the signs inviting visitors to hunt for sapphires for a fee. And there were other signs—of lapidary shops offering to turn those finds into custom-made jewelry.

"How did you possibly guess?" Will laughed as Ruby finally succeeded in knocking him over.

Clem went to kneel again by the stream. "Well," she began as she scooped up more rocks, "for one thing, you don't talk like you're from around here. For another thing, you don't dress like you're from around here."

Will, feigning embarrassment, looked down at his clothing. "I'll have you know that wet dog hair is a leading fashion accessory this year."

Clem grinned as Will brushed himself off and came to join her at the water's edge.

"Sorry about that," Clem said. "Ruby can be overly friendly sometimes."

"That's okay," Will said. "I like my women friendly."

Choosing to ignore that remark, Clem continued. "But most of all, you can't be from around here and not know what corundum is. Red corundum is ruby, and all other colors are sapphire. Most of the sapphires around here are pink. Didn't you see the signs about rock hunting and jewelry making in town?"

"I haven't been into town yet," Will explained. "I came straight here from the interstate. I'm on vacation, and I thought I'd do a little hiking." Will mimicked Clem's dredging until he had his own rock pile spread out on the bank.

At least he was not afraid to get his hands dirty, Clem observed. She looked at him from the corner of her eye as he bent to his task, carefully studying each stone before casting it aside.

With her artist's eye, she silently admired his finely sculpted but masculine profile. His brows and lashes were as black as the India ink she liked to sketch with. His full, sensitive mouth reminded her of the picture of Michelangelo's David in one of her art books. *Wonder what* this *guy would look like naked?* she thought, and felt herself blush.

Sensing her gaze on him, Will looked up just in time to see her quickly refocus her attention on a rather ordinary looking rock. He was used to admiring looks from women, and usually did not give them a second thought, but when this one fixed her green eyes on him, it pleased him. Warmed him.

The realization came to him that—unlike the women he met in his Manhattan business and social circles—this one had no idea who he was. Ordinarily, he never knew how much a woman's attraction to him was due to his power, his money, or his fame.

A certain wariness had crept into his relationships with women over the years that had hardened into outright cynicism. This woman, though, unless he missed his guess, was above suspicion—at least so far—so when the warmth of her gaze traveled over him, it was an unexpected turn-on.

Her hair was beginning to dry a little, turning into a mass of corkscrew curls, revealing its true color, a rich red. Rising, she dusted the dirt from her hands and walked over to the stream again, a little higher up the hill, where she had anchored a plastic bottle to keep it cool. *Now there's a real natural beauty,* Will thought. Her skin was fair except for the rosy cheeks, which he'd expect to see on someone who spent a lot of time outdoors. She was obviously smart. Somehow the subject of geology had never seemed so interesting as just now, when she was telling him about the local rocks.

She was quite a contrast from the women he was used to—professional women with their briefcases and power suits. Clem looked as comfortable as if she'd always lived outdoors, like some mythological wood nymph come to life. The thought made him chuckle.

Clem saw his expression and drew herself up defensively. "What's so funny?" She recapped the bottle and put her hand on her hip, giving Will a suspicious stare.

"Nothing, I was just . . ." Will began. "Nothing." She offered him the water bottle before returning to her rocks, but he waved it off. "So, what do you do with your time around here besides look for rocks and wallow in mountain streams?" he asked.

"I'm a lapidary." Clem washed the mud off a rock. "I cut and polish rocks and make them into jewelry. I work at my uncle's shop, about three miles from here."

"Do you always come out here in the woods to find your own rocks?"

"Sometimes," Clem said, "But mostly folks bring me the ones they find, and I make them into something nice."

"Hmmm. A prospector named Clem," Will said, chuckling. "Didn't somebody write a song about you?"

"That was a little before my time." Clem looked over at him. He had stopped washing rocks and sat cross-legged, watching her with an amused smile.

He thinks he's come across a real country bumpkin, she thought.

"I'm counting on finding a big ruby around here," Clem said, dumping more rocks on the bank. "Maybe even a vein that I can mine."

"Are you serious?" Will's eyes widened.

"Yes, I'm serious," Clem said. Something in his tone put her on the defensive, and the way he was looking at her made her feel like the featured attraction at a sideshow. She sat back and brushed the dirt off her knees. "It was right here, a little farther down along Cherokee Creek, that one of the biggest sapphires in North America was found back in the thirties."

"So how come this mountain isn't covered with commercial mining equipment?" Will asked, his eyes narrowing.

"There were some mining companies here at one time, but they didn't find many large, gem-quality stones, so they gave up. Now they have a few mines open where tourists pay a fee to look through buckets of rocks dug out from the hillsides."

"What happens when you find this strike? How do you get permission to get the rocks out?"

"I just make arrangements with the owner of the

land to lease the mineral rights, or I pay them royalties on the wholesale value of the rocks."

Will looked around him as if he hadn't really seen his surroundings clearly before. "So, unlike those mining companies, you haven't given up on finding more big rubies and sapphires?"

"Nope."

"Why not?"

" 'Cause I need the money," Clem said with a sigh. "My uncle's lapidary shop is way behind with the taxes. And besides that, I feel lucky."

"Lucky?" Will crawled over to the bank to face her again.

Clem looked up at him, exasperated. He was wearing that bemused look again, and it was starting to get on her nerves. "Yeah, lucky," Clem began. "You know—four-leaf clovers, horseshoes, rabbits' feet— luck. *Why* are you looking at me as if I'm a Martian?"

Will laughed good-naturedly. "Because you are. That is, I've never seen anyone quite like you. Here you are digging in the dirt and mud on this hillside, looking for gems like a leprechaun looking for a pot of gold. What are the chances of that?"

Flustered, Clem glared at him. He propped one elbow on the mossy ground and leaned back, having lost interest in helping her look through the rocks.

Will plucked a piece of straw and chewed it thoughtfully. "I guess I don't believe in luck."

"You don't *what?*"

"I don't believe in luck." Will almost laughed at her appalled expression. "You see, I'm in the business of helping people invest their money, so I've seen every get-rich-quick scheme in the book. I've seen people throw their money away on all kinds of far-out business ventures, just because they felt lucky.

And after all my years in the business, I can count on one hand the times that somebody made money because of luck and not because of hard work, research, and wise decision making."

It was Clem's turn to look at Will as if he were from outer space. As she sat back and stared at him, Ruby came bounding back from wherever she had gone exploring, having been attracted by Clem's rising voice. Seeing that her mistress was not in distress, Ruby pawed idly at the rock pile, sending the rocks rolling here and there.

"Well, I must say, that's pretty sad." Clem looked at him with genuine pity. "You know, you could learn a thing or two . . . hey!"

Clem had glanced down at Ruby's pawing just in time to see her uncover something familiar. "Ruby, you found it! You made me lose it, and then you found it again. What a good girl!" Clem hugged the dog tightly, ruffling the fur on her neck.

Will suddenly went slackjawed, causing the piece of straw to fall to the ground. Finding that rock again was like finding a needle in a haystack, but she'd done it. Maybe he would have to amend his feelings about luck. On the other hand, perhaps this particular young woman led a charmed life. He certainly wouldn't mind getting to know her better.

Still hugging the dog, Clem handed the stone to Will. "See?" she said triumphantly.

Will took the stone and marveled at it, turning it over and over in his hands. There were the triangles, just as she'd said, and it was pink, all right. Suddenly, a wicked gleam came into his eye. He calmly put the stone in the breast pocket of his khaki shirt, settled back onto the grass again, and grinned mischievously.

"Hey, what's the idea?" Clem demanded.

   Will patted his pocket and changed his expression
to one of feigned innocence. "I guess since this is my
land," he said, pausing for effect as Clem's mouth
dropped open in surprise, "this is my rock."

TWO

His rock, huh? Clem put her hand to a dusty pane on one of the cabin's front windows and wiped away enough dirt to see out. After his revelation, Will had asked her to join him for lunch at "his place." She could hardly refuse, under the circumstances. She had to get that rock back. It wasn't extremely valuable by most people's standards, but in her present financial straits, it was certainly too valuable to give away.

She turned around and watched him as he took cold cuts, lettuce, and tomato from the ice chest and arranged paper plates and plastic flatware on the rustic wooden table. Ruby lounged lazily in front of the fireplace, her chin resting on her forelegs.

"Well, you set a nice table, but you're not much of a housekeeper," Clem observed dryly. She bent over and blew the dust off a pedestal table near the window.

"What can I say? It's the maid's day off." Will glanced around. "From what I understand, this cabin hasn't been used in several years, probably since the former owner died."

"This place used to belong to old Mr. Mitchell. I thought his son still owned it."

"You knew the Mitchells?"

"We were neighbors for years and years. They said I could prospect here all I wanted. My property and my uncle's is over on the western border of this place. That's where the shop is, too."

Clem walked over to the pile of electronic equipment in one corner. There was a computer, fax machine, and a few gizmos she didn't recognize. "What are you going to do with this stuff?" she asked.

"As soon as they turn the electricity and phone service back on, I'll be able to conduct business from right here," Will said, beckoning Clem to the table.

"What kind of business are you in?"

"I do a lot of different things. Right now, I guess you could call me an investment banker."

A banker. Clem had had her fill of bankers lately. All the local ones had turned down her pleas for a business loan. "So you're going to be here for a while?" Clem asked, stepping over the bench-style seat facing Will.

"I figured I would stay two or three weeks, just for a change of pace. You know, to escape the rat race."

Clem studied him as he began making his sandwich. "How did you come by this land, anyway?" She reached into the bread bag and removed two thick, moist pieces of white bread.

"I bought it from the estate of its late owner."

Ruby raised her head and sniffed as the aroma of the cold cuts reached her sensitive nose. She sat down on the floor beside the table, and Will gave her a couple of slices of baked ham.

"Why?" Clem said, raising the sandwich to her mouth.

Will gave Ruby a piece of bread. "Why what?"

"Why did you buy the land?" Clem took a bite of

her sandwich and looked at Will expectantly. He returned her look with a puzzled one of his own.

"For the investment, of course," he said. "Want some chips?"

"No thanks," Clem said, chewing slowly. "Buy low and sell high, huh?"

"That's the idea."

"So are you going to sell the land right away, or hold onto it for a while?"

"I haven't decided yet." Will took a drink of his cola and looked at her thoughtfully for a moment. "What do you think I should do?"

Clem rolled her eyes. "Let me see, what should you do with the land? Okay, here's the deal. You donate it to the government to be used as a national park, with the provision that I have sole mineral rights for life."

Will pretended to choke on his drink and laughed. "That's quite a plan."

"Well, you asked," Clem said, then grew serious again. "What's really going to happen to this land, city boy?"

"I'm not sure. All I know is that a group of investors say they are about to make me an offer. They're not my regular clients, so I don't know what they'll do with the land—develop it in some way, I expect."

Clem abruptly put her sandwich down and lowered her eyes. Will looked at the woman across the table from him and wondered why he was suddenly being overcome by feelings of guilt. He had made scores of real estate deals and never thought about the consequences. He had never done anything unethical, and as far as he knew, nobody had ever suffered as a result of one of his deals, so why did he feel like he was about to build a widows' and orphans' home on a toxic waste dump?

"You know, just because the land is being sold doesn't mean that someone's going to come in here and cover the mountains with fast food joints. Maybe these people will sell you the mineral rights. I'd be glad to speak to them for you, when and if I close the deal."

Clem looked up again. "I'd appreciate that," she said, a look of desperation in her eyes. "But there's no guarantee that you'll get them to agree to it, is there?"

"Well, no," Will said. He watched her silently and cursed himself for his guilt feelings. This girl, so charming and lively this morning, now looked beaten. He felt an odd protectiveness toward her, something he seldom, if ever, felt for anyone. In Manhattan he saw homeless, disenfranchised people every day. Sure, he donated money to the homeless shelters, and not a small amount, either, but he had become hardened to the sight of people in need, like many. Why was this girl's pain making him feel so uncomfortable?

"Aren't you going to finish your lunch?" he asked.

"I'm not hungry anymore. Come on, Ruby." Clem hastily gathered the belongings that she had put on the floor next to the computer gadgets. If he sold the land to a group of anonymous investors, she could be denied access to it. She was convinced that the rock she was looking for was here on this land. *Think!* she commanded herself. Then she saw something that gave her an idea.

"Listen," Will began, as if not knowing what to say.

Just as Clem reached the cabin door, he caught up with her and caught her arm, turning her to face him. "Wait. You forgot the sapphire. I was only kidding when I took it before." He removed it from his pocket and held it out to her.

Clem looked at the stone and back at him. "You keep it," she said. "You see, I believe in luck. And it looks like my luck might have just run out."

With that, Clem left him at the door of the cabin and started down the trail with Ruby trotting at her heels. When she was almost to the main road, she sat down on a log. "Take a load off, girl," she told Ruby, and started rummaging through the canvas bag into which she'd hastily thrown her tools and water bottle in Will's cabin.

Ruby sat obediently as Clem pulled a small, flat metal box from the bag. "You know something, Ruby? We haven't seen the last of Will Fletcher. And we haven't given up on mining this land, either." She turned the object over and over in her hands.

"They're making these things smaller and smaller these days," she observed idly. "You know what this is, Ruby?"

Ruby continued to thump her tail against the log.

"This is a modem. And without this, he can't connect his computer to the phone. And without his computer hookup, it's going to be tough for him to conduct business as usual. He could use the phone by itself to make a real estate deal, but I get the feeling a deal isn't that imminent . . . yet."

Swiping the modem would free up a day or so of his time, and give her a chance to think of a plan. She thought she just might have an idea already.

Clem sat at her workbench early the next morning examining a rough sapphire brought to her by a customer. Unable to concentrate on her work, she put down the stone and rubbed her eyes. The plan that had come to her yesterday was crystallizing in her mind. If things went as she anticipated, she could expect a visit from Will any time now.

His business was investing money for people, so she'd just convince him to invest some of it in her shop. Clem didn't know much about finance, but she was pretty sure she had a lot of work to do to convince him that the shop was worth backing. She'd already tipped her hand that she was having a difficult time.

As she pondered the problem, she took up a pencil and made marks on the rock to guide her cutting. A delicate process, stonecutting, but no more delicate than the task she had to accomplish when Will came through that door. She hated having to ask anyone for money, even bankers, but she had little choice.

"Coffee's ready," Uncle Jess called from the tiny kitchen in the back of the shop. As she went to get her cup, Jess said, "You've been awfully quiet this morning. Is everything all right?"

"I've just been thinking, that's all." Clem smiled at the old man. Nobody else knew her the way he did, at least not since her mother had left. She didn't want to share her plan with him yet, in case it fell through.

Her smile turned into a frown of concern as Jess picked up the jar of powdered coffee creamer and struggled to open it. The pain of the effort was plain on his face.

"Let me do that for you." Clem gently took the jar from him, opened it easily, and returned it.

"Thank you, child. My arthritis is acting up."

Clem bit her lip and turned away. Jess's condition had gotten so bad that the simplest household chores were becoming difficult for him. She went to check on him often, just to make sure he was okay. The cabin Clem's father had left her was only a hundred yards or so from Jess's, so it was no trouble, but it broke her heart to see his condition deteriorating.

The worst of it, though, was that Jess could no longer do what he loved most—cut and polish stones. While Clem's own talent was well-known, she couldn't produce enough on her own to keep the shop going. She suspected that he had only kept the shop open this long so that she could have her own place as long as possible.

As Clem returned to her workbench, Jess looked after her sadly and rubbed his throbbing wrist. With Clem's skills as a lapidary and silversmith, any one of the shops in the valley would be glad to have her work for them, but she would not be tied down by a time clock.

Whenever the spirit moved her, she went prospecting, exploring, or heaven knew where. When people spoke of Clem Harper, they used terms like "free spirit." Jess himself always just said, "The girl's plumb wild."

No, Jess thought, leaning against the door frame watching her and sipping his coffee, *Clem would not be tied down by anybody.* That included a man. The best-looking young men in the county had all tried to court her. She'd dated a few, but none could get her to the altar. The young men had promise, but they also had dreams that took them beyond the mountains, and Clem would not hear of leaving. "I'll never let a man take me out of these mountains like Mama did," she'd once said.

Jess sighed. She belonged with some nice man, hav-

ing his babies, but not just any man. He would have
to be a mighty strong one.

Jess downed the last of his coffee. "I'm going to
go back up to the house," he said, and ambled toward the back door.

Knowing how painful it was for him, Clem winced
as she heard him making his way slowly down the
back steps. She had to smile, though, when she heard
the whine of his three-wheeled scooter as he started
the engine. Jess liked to ride the short distance between the shop and his house on his "tricycle," as
he called it.

Clem picked up the sign she'd just lettered by hand
that morning and set it on the front display case in
a prominent position. The sign read:

Guided Rock Hunting Tours.
Camping Gear Rental Extra.

If she couldn't produce enough jewelry by herself
to keep the shop open, then she'd just offer additional services. That should prove to Will that she
had initiative, at least. Clem looked at the sign and
bit her lip. She had no idea if it would be enough.

She only led guided trips once in a while, prefer-
ring to prospect on her own, free to go wherever she
wanted, anytime she wanted. But to become a businesswoman, she was going to have to do whatever was
necessary. Maybe demonstrating her versatility would
help prove to Will that she could make a go of it.

It wasn't going to be easy. She didn't know much
about running a business. Uncle Jess had always handled the financial side of things. All she knew was
that the taxes were due soon, and she didn't have
the money to pay them. The only things she had to

offer were her talent and determination. Somehow she would have to convince Will that was enough. He had said he was on vacation, and that he wanted to do some hiking. If she could get him alone on a two-day prospecting trip, he could see for himself that she was competent.

At the same time, she could grill him on what he looked for in a business investment and then tailor her sales pitch accordingly. By that time, he'd be so in love with the mountains and with rock hunting that he'd give her the loan.

Clem heard a faint noise and looked over at her dog, who was asleep in front of the potbellied stove. Ruby squirmed and whined for a few seconds, until Clem bent to stroke the velvety fur between the dog's ears. Whatever doggie demons pursued Ruby in her nightmare were vanquished. Her tail thumped against the floor twice and she was still, her peaceful sleep restored.

Clem found herself wishing there was someone who could calm her own fears and make the bad dreams go away—like the one in which she had to give up the way of life she loved. And the other one— the one about the city.

Shivering, Clem took her tools, a block of wax, and her coffee, and went out on the porch to wait.

Clem sat cross-legged on the porch of the lapidary shop, the small chunk of wax in her left hand and a carving tool in her right. She looked up from her work from time to time to revel in the beauty of the mountain morning. Even though wildflowers dotting the roadside signaled that winter had turned to spring, the air was still cool. In the distance, tendrils of smoke rose lazily from a dozen chimneys on the hillsides here and there.

Clem's concentration was broken by the crunch of tires on the gravel driveway. She took a couple of deep breaths to calm herself as the Mercedes sedan turned off the main road and made its way up the winding drive. *It's him,* she thought, and fought the urge to straighten her hair, which was piled carelessly on her head. She had been so preoccupied this morning that she'd forgotten to make herself presentable.

As Will's car pulled to a stop beside the cabin, Clem bent her head over her work again and pretended to concentrate. Out of the corner of her eye, she saw Will get out of the car. He wore a red designer polo shirt, jeans, athletic shoes, and a guarded expression.

"Good morning," Will said as he reached the bottom step of the porch.

"Good morning," Clem replied, glancing up at him briefly.

"What's that you're doing?" Will put his foot on the first step and leaned forward, resting his hands on his knee.

"You know us country folk," Clem said, "We like to pass the time by sitting on the porch whittling."

The nearness of him as he leaned toward her made her heart pound. Her hands even started to shake a little. *Not a good thing when you're doing delicate work,* she chided herself. His cologne smelled masculine, hypnotic, and expensive.

"Very funny," Will said, grinning. He leaned even closer, trying to get a better look at her work, and at her.

Clem wore cutoff shorts, tennis shoes, and a man's chambray shirt with the sleeves rolled up.

As he casually studied her, Will found himself wondering who the shirt belonged to. The thought made him uncomfortable, and he mentally shook off the feeling.

"I thought maybe you might be carving a jewelry design out of wax so you could make it into silver or gold using centrifugal casting."

"A nice car and brains, too," she said. "How do you know about that?"

"A friend of mine runs an art gallery, and she loves to show jewelry."

Clem looked up at him finally. "A lady brought me a sapphire she found, and wanted me to put it in one of those dragonfly lady settings."

"Dragonfly lady?" Will asked, puzzled.

"You know, a naked dragonfly lady." Clem held up the carving for him to see, but drew it back quickly. "I forgot. The last thing I let you hold, you didn't give back."

Will gave her a contrite look. "Can I see it if I promise to give it back?"

"Well, I suppose." Clem grinned and handed him the wax sculpture. Will sat down on the top step next to her to examine it.

"Oh, yeah, a dragonfly lady," Will said with recognition. "This is a common art nouveau motif."

"I guess in addition to knowing about money and finance, you also know about jewelry and art."

"Only as something some people like to invest in," he said. "As they say, I don't know much about art, but I know what I like." He gave her a long, appreciative look, and was rewarded with a blush.

"I never studied art formally, so I don't know the official names of things. I just call them naked dragonfly ladies, or whatever they happen to be."

Will examined the sculpture again. It was good work. He looked closely at the perfect, womanly shape of the tiny figure and wondered if it were a self-portrait.

"You may not have had any formal training, but you're obviously talented."

His praise gave her another rush of warmth. People told her all the time how talented she was. Why should it seem so much more important coming from him? Maybe it was because she hoped to borrow money from him for the business. Maybe it was because he was from New York, and had a critical eye for art. Or maybe it was because of how he made her feel when he fixed those vivid blue eyes on her.

"My Dad taught me a lot about lapidary before he died, and then Uncle Jess taught me the rest of what I know about rocks. But I taught myself about art from looking at the pictures in art books."

She held out her hand for the sculpture, and he placed it in her palm, letting his fingers linger there a moment. She sighed audibly at his touch and jerked her hand away.

Clem got up quickly and stood leaning against the porch railing looking down at him. "Did you mean what you said before?"

"About what?"

"About only caring about art as something to invest in?"

Will leaned back on one elbow, considering her question carefully. "Actually, I don't like to invest in art myself, and I usually advise my clients against it, too. I guess I don't take the time to appreciate art," he said thoughtfully. "Whenever I go to a gallery, it's usually to meet people. You know, to see and be seen."

Clem stared off into the distance, trying to conjure

up the images of a world she'd only read about and seen on TV and in movies. "I bet you go to fancy art show openings at those ritzy galleries where they serve champagne and stand around talking about the deep meaning in those piles of scrap metal New Yorkers call art."

Clem immediately wondered if her remark had gone too far, but Will laughed so loud the sound echoed through the hollow.

"Oh, so you've been there?" Will said, still chuckling.

Clem shook her head and returned to sit on the top step beside him.

He looked at her thoughtfully. "Have you ever thought about going to New York?"

"No!" Clem said, a little too forcefully. "Why would I want to do that?"

Will paused, as if sensing that he was treading on dangerous ground. "For the same reason everyone else does—to see the world, make your fortune and all that."

"I do fine right here, thank you very much." Biting her lower lip, Clem realized she'd told him just the opposite yesterday.

She saw him studying her and decided to change the subject. "So you go to these galleries to meet people, huh? What kind of people?"

"People with money who might want me to invest it for them."

"Why do you advise them not to invest in art?"

Will leaned back against the post behind him. "Art is such a difficult thing to put a value on. For example, some people might think a painting was God's gift to mankind, and other people might think it was a piece of . . . well, maybe they wouldn't like it. I'll stick to stocks and bonds." They looked at each other for a long moment before he said, "Now you're looking at me as if *I'm* the Martian."

"I've never known anyone quite like you," she said honestly.

His only use for art was to meet people with money to invest, Clem thought sadly. How could a person look at beautiful things and see nothing but means of making money? As she looked at him there in a shaft of morning sun, his hair and eyelashes shone blue-black, his eyes a glittering periwinkle blue. He was a thing of masculine beauty himself, but something was wrong with his soul. She felt sorry for him, and shivered. *Why am I feeling sorry for this guy? He's rich, powerful, good-looking. . . .*

Will gazed up into the pines above their heads as the sun broke from behind some clouds, bathing them both in golden light. He glanced back at Clem, who was looking at him strangely. The sun made a halo out of the wispy tendrils of Titian hair trying to escape the twist atop her head.

Just like an angel, he thought, but what was that emotion in her eyes? Was it sadness? Feeling suddenly uncomfortable, Will decided it was time he came around to the purpose of his visit.

"So you taught yourself about art from studying books?" he asked. "Is that how you taught yourself about computers, too—with books?"

Clem met his steady gaze with an innocent look. "Computers? What makes you think I know anything about computers?"

"Oh, just a hunch. By the way, when you were gathering up your things at the cabin yesterday, did you by any chance happen to see a little flat box—about this big, with lights on it?" Will held his hands up a few inches apart.

"Oh, is it very important?" Clem fluttered her eyelashes slightly.

"It's a device that connects the computer with the phone line," Will explained. "Without it, I can't get stock quotes, my electronic mail, and all the other information I need."

"Can't you go just a few days without knowing what the stock market is doing?" Clem looked at him and made a face.

Will blinked a couple of times. "Well, no."

They stared at each other for what seemed like minutes. She looked at him strangely again, as if he were a new species of insect she'd just caught and pinned to a board for science class.

"Have to take care of business, huh?" Clem said. "Anyway, I haven't seen your modem." She nearly choked on the last swallow of coffee as she realized he'd never mentioned the name of the gizmo.

"Oh, so you *do* know something about computers." Will narrowed his eyes.

"One of my old boyfriends took data processing courses out at the vo-tech school. He taught me a little."

"So where is this old boyfriend now?"

"Atlanta. He's a programmer for a big software company."

Clem saw his face turn hard with displeasure. Did he suspect that she was lying about the modem, or was it something else? She decided it was time to see if he would take the bait for the rock hunting trip.

She held up her coffee cup. "I'm going to have another cup. Would you like some?" she asked brightly.

"Sure."

They rose and entered the shop. Clem left him standing in front of the display case while she went toward the back. "Do you take sugar and cream?"

"No, just black."

Will looked in the glass case and let out a low whistle. Half of the case contained exquisite pins and pendants in silver, gold, and colored gemstones. He judged the pieces to be elegant enough to satisfy the taste of the most sophisticated woman.

The other side of the case contained a virtual menagerie of silver animals with sapphire-studded eyes and tails. The whimsical creatures seemed alive, prowling through a carved and painted wooden forest which was a masterpiece in itself. Will recognized the tiny landscape immediately—it was this very mountain community. *This is her world,* he thought, *and this is the magical way she sees it.*

He halfway expected the fanciful creatures to come to life. He had to laugh when he saw, in one corner, a tiny golden retriever with rubies for eyes. He was so entranced with the jewelry pieces that he almost didn't notice the sign on the case, but his gaze finally came to rest there.

The coffee was already made, so all Clem had to do was pour it, but she fiddled with the cups and spoons for a few seconds to give him time to see the sign. She peeked around the corner and sure enough, he was looking at it. She let her gaze linger a little too long. He glanced up in time to catch her looking at him, and she looked away quickly.

Clem returned with the coffee and beckoned Will to come around behind the display case. He sat in the chair next to her bench and took a sip of the coffee.

"What are you going to do about the modem?" Clem asked. "It's a long way to the nearest computer store."

"I guess I'll just call the office and have them send a new one. It'll probably take a day or so."

"So what are you going to do until then?" Clem idly rearranged the tools on the top of her workbench.

Will smiled pleasantly. "I don't have any formal plans. Do you have any suggestions?"

"Well, you said you wanted to do some hiking. You could go on a rock hunting expedition that would involve plenty of hiking. It's what the area's famous for, you know."

"Sounds like a great idea. When do we start?"

Clem was surprised at how eagerly he agreed to the trip. Perhaps she shouldn't sound too anxious herself. Feigning a concerned look, she said, "The overnight trips I organize are mostly for groups. I don't know if it would be a good idea for me to go out into the woods overnight with a stranger."

"Local tongues will wag, eh?" Will teased.

Clem laughed. "Local gossip is one thing I've never worried about."

"I believe that." He looked at her for a moment and shook his head. "Okay. If you don't think it's a good idea, I guess I can always get another guide."

"Not so fast," Clem said. "I'll take you, and I'll supply all the camping gear . . . but that'll cost extra."

Will looked at her with a deadpan expression long enough to make her wonder if he were going to back out and then said, "Okay. And I promise to behave like a perfect gentleman."

They smiled benignly at each other for a moment

until Will said suddenly, "I guess I should go ahead and call the office. Can I use your phone? They're not coming to connect mine until this afternoon."

"Sure. It's right over there." She pointed to the opposite wall of the shop.

"Thanks."

As he dialed the phone, Clem took a deep breath. She had her chance. She had two days to convince him to help her save the shop. It was going to be tough being alone in the woods with this man for two days—she sensed he was attracted to her. She also knew instinctively that he was trustworthy, though. Her instincts had never been wrong.

Still, it was obvious that Will Fletcher was used to getting exactly what he wanted. She'd just have to try not to let him get any ideas. She'd make sure to keep things strictly business.

She wondered, though, if the greater problem would be keeping herself from getting too attracted to him. She'd been hurt more than once, getting too attached to someone who left to find his fortune elsewhere. A relationship with this guy was clearly out of the question. He already lived in a whole different world.

Slowly, his words to the unseen person on the other end of the line began to invade her consciousness.

"They're pressuring you for an answer from me, are they?" he demanded. His voice had taken on a kind of authoritative tone she'd never heard anyone use. "Well, they'll just have to wait."

As he gave his employee the instructions for sending the modem, she realized that even his posture had changed during the brief conversation. He was no longer relaxed. His lean, muscular frame seemed poised for some kind of conflict to the death.

Clem pictured him in an expensive suit, striding confidently through the corridors of financial power in some Wall Street skyscraper. She could almost hear the choruses of "Good morning, Mr. Fletcher. Good morning, Mr. Fletcher."

As he finished the conversation and turned to face her again, he seemed once more relaxed. He returned to the chair and finished the last of his coffee. "So, Clem, when do we leave?"

"I'll get all the stuff together this afternoon and meet you at your cabin bright and early tomorrow morning."

"Great. See you then. And thanks for the coffee."

They both stood. He looked at her a moment before he turned to go and paused at the display case. "I meant to tell you before," he said. "I really love your work." With that, he smiled and went out the door.

At the bottom of the steps, he turned to look at her again. She was still standing behind her workbench, looking at him mysteriously over the rim of her coffee cup.

What's your plan for me, my darling Clementine?

THREE

The sunrise was barely breaking over the hills when Clem pulled up to Will's cabin in her old Chevy pickup. Gazing to the east to admire the first pink and yellow rays, she jumped down from the cab and Ruby bounded out behind her. The air was clear and cool—just right for a hike, she decided. Uncle Jess's bones and joints were paining him no more than usual, a sure sign of fine weather. A good thing, too, since she wanted this trip to be perfect.

Now, if only the rest of her luck would hold, she should be able to make a good impression on Will. Clem walked to the back of the truck and let down the tailgate so they could unload the gear. As she did, she glanced at the cabin and noticed that there was no light on inside.

"Looks like the city boy's not awake yet." Clem reached down to pat the dog's head. Anticipating a trek through the woods, Ruby wagged her tail so vigorously that her whole body swayed. "Guess we'll have to go wake him up, or we'll miss the best part of the morning."

Walking up the cabin's steps with Ruby at her heels, Clem knocked on the door a couple of times and waited. After a few seconds, she heard footsteps on the floorboards, accompanied by a muffled groan. Then Will opened the door.

"Hey, I thought I told you we were going to leave bright and early and here you are"—Clem paused in midsentence—"in the altogether."

Will was naked except for the small pillow he held in a strategic location.

Clem froze. A voice in her head somewhere said she should look away. It would be the ladylike thing to do. But she stared. What was that old expression? *In all his glory?* Well, that was the word, all right. *Glorious.*

Her gaze took him in all at once and then started over, from the top. Broad, square shoulders sat atop a well-defined chest and biceps. She marvelled at his abdomen, taut with little rectangular washboard muscles. Narrow hips and powerful-looking legs completed the package.

A deep, rich tan covered his entire body, except for a thin strip of paler flesh on either side of the pillow. Crisp, black hair blanketed his chest. It grew coarser and thicker the lower it went, until it disappeared in a V shape beneath the pillow.

Blasted pillow, Clem thought.

Though Will was blinking the sleep from his eyes and squinting into the rising sun, his expression hinted that he could still discern her appreciative stare. His insolent grin confirmed the fact.

Clem came back to reality and colored deeply as her gaze returned to his face, which now wore a still sleepy but more amused expression. He grinned again, obviously aware of the effect his masculine glory was having on her. Clem glanced down at Ruby. The dog had stopped wagging her tail and had started to pant.

As Will leaned against the door frame, Clem felt her face radiating heat. Was it from embarrassment, or something else? she wondered. Nobody should look this good just getting out of bed.

Clem finally looked away and began to stammer, trying desperately to think of something, *anything*, to say to cover the awkward moment. "I figured when you said you wanted to go camping that you'd like to get back to nature, but I didn't realize you meant to go to this extreme."

Will grinned. "You mean we're actually going to wear *clothing* on this trip?"

"For the sake of the burrs and the briars, I'm afraid I have to insist."

"Oh, all right. Excuse me a minute and I'll get myself decent."

As he disappeared into the cabin Clem sat down rather heavily on the porch. She hadn't realized how weak her knees were. The sight of a man had never affected her this way. As she stroked Ruby's head, she thought about the dozens of books on classical art that she'd studied throughout the years. In all those pages and pages of the finest representations of the human form, she thought, she'd never seen a male body as perfect as Will's.

He had just the right amount of muscles, she decided. He wasn't all lumpy like the competitive bodybuilders and weight lifters she saw on TV. He just looked—*strong*, that was the word. As an artist, she wished she could draw him in the nude. She could just see him reclining on a bearskin rug, with her at her easel in front of a roaring fire. The thought made her go tingly all over.

As she heard his footsteps approaching the door,

she hastily grabbed the topographic map she'd stuck into her back pocket and pretended to study it.

"Do you like this getup better?" Will stepped out of the cabin doorway. He wore another expensive looking hiking outfit, and carried a bundle of clothing and other items for the trip.

"Yes, much." Clem wondered if he knew she was lying.

"You said you'd be here bright and early, but I didn't figure you meant the crack of dawn. Do you get up this early every day?"

"We country folk like to get up with the chickens. Besides, we have a lot of ground to cover today."

She headed for the truck, and Will followed. In the back of the truck, Clem had stored items for two packs. There were two sleeping bags, two folded air mattresses, two sheets of plastic, and plastic bags containing food and other supplies. There was also a frying pan and a small cookstove.

Clem pointed to the plastic bags he was holding. "What's that?"

Will held out one of the packages. "This one is beef Stroganoff. I got them at the outdoor store where I got the clothes."

Clem took the package and squeezed it gingerly. "Hmm, twelve dollars and fifty cents. I sure hope it's good." She handed the packages back.

"Just like Mom used to make." Will grinned.

Clem turned back toward the truck and removed what looked like a small saddlebag. Bending down, she attached it to Ruby's harness.

"Ruby always carries her own weight," she explained. "There's dry kibble in there for her dinner. I don't want her going off and finding her own game."

"You think of everything, don't you?"

"I try."

When Clem was satisfied that they had everything they needed and their packs were assembled, they started out. They had only gone a little way up the trail when they came to a clearing in the forest.

Sunlight poured into the little glade from the east, as if through a cathedral window. The canopy of trees all around the edges of the clearing created a magical little enclave through which ran a softly babbling stream. The stream was dotted by rocks smoothed by the unending trek of the water, a dance as ancient as the forest itself.

The clearing was carpeted by a growth of soft, thick grass of the greenest green, and a profusion of flowers grew along the creek and the edge of the woods.

"What a beautiful spot," Will said. "It seems almost . . . otherworldly."

Clem looked at him appreciatively. "That's a good word for it. I always thought of it as a magical place. I used to love to come here as a kid. It was always a kind of sanctuary for me. The deer like to come here and drink, also rabbits, squirrels, all kinds of wildlife. And if you think it's gorgeous at dawn, you should see it at sunset."

"I can see why you love it so much."

Clem took a last look at her special place, then led Will back to the trail. Ruby repeatedly bounded up the trail to inspect what lay ahead and then ran back to Clem and Will, as if to make sure they were still behind her. From time to time she left the path, on the trail of a chipmunk or lizard, but she always returned before the hikers got out of her sight.

"I'm going to go out on a limb here," Clem said,

looking sidelong at Will, "and guess that you've never been camping before."

"Don't tell me. It was the dried Stroganoff that tipped you off."

He looked over at Clem, her hair pulled back from her face. She seemed very capable, but she had a soft quality too, a sweetness—not necessarily innocence, though.

Clem talked about the mountains, pointing out the different examples of flora and fauna. As they rounded a bend in the trail, they saw a squirrel about thirty feet away make a peculiar horizontal leap from the ground to a nearby pine.

"Did you see that squirrel?" Will exclaimed, pointing excitedly. "He . . . he . . . teleported over to that tree."

"He sure did, didn't he?" Clem said calmly.

"I didn't know squirrels could defy the laws of physics."

"They can when a snake slithers up to them."

Will stopped in his tracks. "There's a snake over there?"

"I'd say there's about a ninety percent chance."

"Hmm. I think I could make that jump too, if I saw a snake." He walked quickly to catch up with Clem. "Just when I'm starting to get a warm, fuzzy feeling about communing with nature, you remind me that there are snakes out here."

"There are plenty."

"What kinds?"

Clem shrugged. "I don't know. All kinds, I suppose."

Will looked right and left. "What, in your opinion, is the absolute worst kind of snake in this part of the world, exactly?"

Clem looked thoughtful. "I'd have to say the eastern diamondback rattler."

"Rattlesnakes? Here? I thought they were only out west."

"Oh, they're here, too. They're a thick, big-bodied snake." Clem made a circle of her thumb and forefinger. They lacked a couple of inches touching. "You don't have to worry. They're very shy, and will go to great lengths not to bite you. That's what the rattles are for—to scare you off."

"I should think they would work pretty well in that regard. They'd certainly work on me. It's not that I don't have to deal with snakes in my job, you understand. Only they're the two-legged kind, the snake in the grass variety."

Clem laughed. "I'll bet you deal with some rats, too."

"That's for sure. There are some dirty rats on Wall Street. But that's a whole different world. It's the wildlife here in the forest that concerns me right now."

"Snakes and bugs and bears. Oh, my," Clem chanted in a singsong voice and leaned near him dramatically.

"Bears? You didn't say there would be any bears."

"I didn't say there wouldn't be any bears."

"You're not kidding, are you?"

"Does a bear live in the woods?"

Will gave her a wicked grin. "With all these potential dangers out here in the wilderness, I insist that you stay as close as possible to protect me." He laughed as Clem rolled her eyes. "I'm not used to this environment."

"It ain't the dark side of the moon," she said. "It's just the woods."

Will took in his surroundings, from the blue Carolina sky overhead to the dark earth at his feet. It occurred to him that this was the first time in a long time that he wasn't in absolute control of his situation. He made it his business to know all the cards on the table. No surprises. Now he was walking through a forest full of God-knew-what with only a rock collector and her dog for guides. Anything, anything at all, could be around the next bend in the trail. He had to admit, it was a thrill. Maybe this trip was just the kind of challenge he needed. Either that, or he'd completely lost his mind.

"Do you think we're likely to see a bear?"

"You never know." Clem nonchalantly kicked a pine cone out of her path. "Thing is, they've just come out of hibernation, and they'll be mighty hungry."

Will reached behind his head and patted the bulging backpack. "Something tells me I didn't bring enough beef Stroganoff."

They both laughed as they dodged some briars that crowded their path. "I'll bet you know a lot about animals, having grown up here in the mountains."

"I do love my critters," Clem said in her best country bumpkin voice, and was rewarded with Will's warm laughter. "I've had all kinds of pets—squirrels, raccoons, a bear, a 'possum."

Will laughed incredulously "How'd you get all these wild pets?"

"Well, for example, the 'possum got into my grandmother's kitchen through a hole in the floor where the water pipes came in. Grandma was sitting at the kitchen table one night drinking a cup of coffee and she saw him out of the corner of her eye, sauntering across the floor as pretty as you please."

"What did Grandma do?"

"Well, first she almost had a conniption fit, because

she thought it was the biggest rat she'd ever seen. But then she realized it was a baby 'possum, so she called me. She figured since I had a way with animals I might be able to find a way to catch him."

"And did you?"

"Yep. I saw him hiding in an old coffeepot on the pantry floor, so I slammed the lid on him and took him outside. I tamed him and kept him as a pet for a while after that. I eventually let him go, though. It was the best thing to do for him, but I missed him. I never could bring myself to eat 'possum again."

Clem smiled at the memory, and then her face took on a stricken look. Glancing briefly at Will, she cast her gaze down at the forest floor. Her face colored, and he would have sworn that it was from shame.

"What's wrong?"

"I don't like admitting I've ever eaten 'possum, that's all."

The significance of this dawned on Will after a moment. 'Possum must be something rural people ate only as a last resort. She must have been terribly poor.

"Talk about your exotic pets," Will said, acting as if he hadn't noticed her discomfort. "I'll bet you could charm the birds right out of the trees, wild child."

He reached above their heads and plucked a stem of wisteria blossoms off a low-hanging vine. Leaning over to her, he tucked the fragrant lavender flower behind Clem's ear, then let his fingers glide along her cheek to her chin. She fixed him with a look so tender that he made an involuntary sound that was part sigh, part growl, and part pure, primitive male possessiveness.

If Clem noticed the sound she didn't let on. She launched into another story as they continued along the trail. He listened in quiet fascination, his attention held fast by the words she spoke and by the way she spoke them. She was a natural storyteller. Not only that, but the dappled sunlight filtering through the canopy of trees did wonderful things to her alabaster skin, and turned her eyes a deep forest-green.

To his delight, she regaled him with story after story about growing up in the mountains. She recounted more of her "critter" stories, as she called them, as well as local legends, Indian myths, and mountain lore. He couldn't remember when he'd been as well entertained. It seemed to him as if no time at all had passed before they'd reached another small clearing beside a stream.

"Hungry?" Clem asked, squinting as they came out of the shade and into the bright sunlight.

"Yes, I suppose I am. But how do you know it's lunchtime?" Will couldn't help noticing that she didn't wear a wristwatch. In fact, he doubted there was anything he hadn't noticed about her, including the way her T-shirt stretched tight across her breasts as she shrugged off her backpack.

"What difference does it make? I don't eat according to a time schedule. I eat when I get hungry. But if you need proof that it's noon before we have lunch, surely even in prep schools they teach you what *that* means." Clem pointed to the sky.

The sun was directly overhead.

Will put his hands on his hips and shot her a look of consternation as she unzipped a pocket in her pack. He didn't know if he was annoyed more by his ignorant slip of mind or by her last remark.

"What makes you think I'm the product of a prep school?" he demanded.

She turned and tossed him a sandwich wrapped in waxed paper. "I call them as I see them."

Neatly catching the sandwich, he studied the curves she displayed as she bent over her pack again to retrieve her water bottle. "What else can you tell about me?"

"I can tell you're somebody important, powerful even. Somebody used to giving orders." As she headed toward the stream, Clem's last remark was almost drowned out by the sound of the rushing water. "Someone born with a silver spoon in his mouth."

So she thought she had him all figured out, did she? Well, in that regard she wasn't much different from most people, but most people didn't know his true background. He preferred to keep it that way—with business associates, anyway. In her case he thought he might come clean, just to teach her a lesson.

"So you can tell that just by the way I look, huh?"

Clem had taken her lunch to the edge of the stream and crawled onto a boulder that jutted out over the water. "Not just that," she said as she settled herself. "It's also because of what you said you do for a living, and how you talked to that person on the phone yesterday."

"And how was that?" Will joined her on the sun-warmed rock.

Clem eyed him thoughtfully for a moment before continuing. "Like someone to be reckoned with."

Will unwrapped the sandwich, watching her out of the corner of his eye so as not to miss the effect his next words would have on her. "What would you say if I told you that I grew up almost as poor as you did?"

Clem stopped chewing and looked at him incredulously. "You're kidding."

"Nope. I never went to private school, didn't get a car when I turned sixteen, and had to work my way through college. In fact, there were times when my folks didn't know where the next month's rent money was coming from."

"But you seem so . . . cultured, so . . . refined."

Suppressing a smile, Will said, "My family *used* to have money. Lots of it. But in the last couple of generations, they let it slip through their fingers."

"How'd they do that?"

"Bad investments mostly. Pie-in-the-sky stuff." Will took a bite of his sandwich and chewed thoughtfully for a moment before continuing. "They were dreamers, you see. Totally impractical when it came to money, and most everything else, for that matter."

Clem looked out over the water for a few moments as Will finished his lunch. Just when he thought she'd tired of this thread of conversation, she asked, "Were they happy?"

Will couldn't have said why, but this struck him as an odd question, irrelevant somehow. He knew the answer without having to think twice. "Yes," he said. "Oh, yes. They were happy."

Clem smiled, seemingly satisfied. "Let's take a siesta. We've hiked a long way today." Folding her arms behind her head, she lay back on the rock. She looked as comfortable stretched out on the rock as if she were lying on a downy mattress.

Will followed suit, closing his eyes. He hadn't noticed how tired he was. Yawning, he realized they must have hiked several miles. The warmth of the sun on his face, combined with the soothing sounds of the babbling water, relaxed him. There was something about Clem's presence beside him that made him feel a kind of contentment that he couldn't remember ever having felt before. Within a few minutes, he'd reached a pleasant, trance-like state between consciousness and sleep.

In his mental haze, the image of his mother came to him. She was sitting in the window seat of her bedroom in the first house he could remember living in. She was young, in her mid-twenties, about the age Clem was now, and she was plainly happy. His father was sitting beside her, whispering softly—words of love, Will thought, or rather, felt. The look his mother gave her young husband was one of love and devotion bordering on the spiritual. It was as if they completed one another.

His throat tightening, he found himself wondering, for the first time in his life, if any woman would ever look at him like that—as if she couldn't bear to look away? As if he was at the center of her world, and the union they made was perfection?

Even in his state of near-hypnosis, Will could feel Clem's gaze on him. Turning his head toward her, he opened his eyes. She regarded him intently, with eyes turned sea green in the sunlight. As she realized he'd caught her looking at him, a tinge of embarrassment crept into her expression, only to be replaced by a lazy grin.

"I'll bet you never had to eat 'possum," she drawled.

For their campsite, Clem selected a flat, grassy area farther up the stream. As Clem unloaded her pack, Will paused to admire the idyllic spot. A nearby waterfall made the scene look like a picture postcard, and provided a pleasing, shooshing sound.

"What do you think?" she asked, following his gaze.

"It's almost as beautiful as the first spot you showed me."

"I'll make a nature lover out of you yet," she said, grinning.

"I think you've already accomplished that."

They pitched the tents quickly and stowed the rest of the gear inside, except for a small pick and two wooden boxes. The boxes were simple wooden frames about a foot square with what looked like window screen stretched across the bottom, making them into sieves.

"A basin next to a waterfall is good for finding rocks," Clem explained as she led Will to the stream. Using the pick, she loosened some rocks and mud from the streambed and dumped a portion of it into the screen box she handed to him.

"Now just swish the box around in the water, and the mud and dirt will wash through the screen. Then sort through the rocks until you find one that looks like the one I found the other day."

Will did as he was told while Clem walked farther up the creek to find rocks of her own. He watched her as she removed her shoes and socks and waded out into the shallow stream. In the bright sunlight, her image seemed to shimmer, giving the impression that she was walking on the silvery water.

It struck him again that she was like some mythical creature—a water nymph come to life, completely unaware of how alluring she was. Her tales of taming wild animals had added to her mystique, giving her a near supernatural air, and yet she seemed so unaffected—as if she assumed everyone had bears as pets.

"Well, are you impressed?"

Will took a deep breath as a breeze caught her hair, caressed it gently, and let it settle about her shoulders again. "Oh, yes."

"I told you you'd love it."

"Love what?"

"Panning for sapphires, of course."

"Of course."

Clem gave him a look of puzzled concern, as if he had been struck by temporary insanity. Perhaps he had been. He didn't believe he had ever been this enchanted by a woman. It was as if she had charmed him the way she charmed her animals. The idea was so ridiculous it made him chuckle. "They're coming to take me away," he muttered under his breath.

Clem watched him as he worked. He seemed to be faraway, somehow, but the looks he gave her were unnerving, as if he'd never seen anything quite like her. With her past experience, she didn't particularly enjoy close scrutiny. If anyone looked at her too closely, she felt as if they were looking for something to ridicule.

She wanted to think this man wasn't like that—he'd been nice so far—but he was so different, so sophisticated and worldly. He worked on Wall Street, for goodness sake. He probably thought she was straight out of *Li'l Abner.*

He might be a city boy, but he looked as if he belonged here. He looked positively rugged, down on one knee by the stream, too rugged to be a desk jockey. *You didn't get muscles like that from pushing buttons on a speakerphone.* He probably worked out at some swank Manhattan club.

They worked in companionable silence for more than an hour before Will shouted, "I've got one!"

Clem came running through the stream, splashing as she went. "You sure do," she said, as he held the rock up for her inspection. "Nice one, too. Ought to make you a good tie tack or something." She handed back the small rock.

"So how much do you think it's worth?"

Clem sat on a rock in the stream and bent over to wash the mud off her hands. "I don't know."

"As a professional, what would be your best guess?"

"Depends on what you could get somebody to pay for it," she said thoughtfully.

"I know *that.*" Will gave her an exasperated look. "If I took this rock to a jeweler in New York, how much would he give me for it?"

Clem flipped her hair over her shoulder. "Oh, a jeweler wouldn't buy that rock. It's not clear enough. But I can still make it into something nice."

Will squeezed his eyes shut. When he began to speak, it was slowly and deliberately, as if to an obstinate child. "Okay, let's say that you did make a tie tack out of it. What would you charge for it?"

Clem frowned at his tone of voice. Nudging a rock with her toe, she said, "It's hard to say."

"Evidently so," Will said, splashing water on his face. After a moment, he looked up at her again, droplets of water clinging to his coal-black lashes. "But I'm going to get a straight answer out of you about this rock if it's the last thing I do."

The look of cool determination on his face was the same as when he'd been on the phone in the shop—no nonsense, all business. Clem returned his level gaze, determined to stand her ground. "It's not that easy to say what I could charge for a piece of jewelry.

Money matters are not always as cut-and-dried as they are on Wall Street. When you make your living by selling something you created with your own hands, you go by more than carats and pennyweights of gold and silver. You go by your heart."

"I forgot, you're an *artist.*"

Clem wondered what was behind his emphasis on the word "artist." His eyes narrowed, and his jaw set itself in a hard line. Drawing herself up, she said, "And what's wrong with that?"

"Don't get me started." He stood up and dried his hands on his shirt.

Clem raised a brow and crossed her arms in front of her. "No, I insist."

Will paused for a moment, looking at her as if trying to decide if she could handle what he had to tell her. "Let's just say that I've seen a lot of artistic concerns go down the tubes because of just that kind of attitude. You've already said your own business is in trouble. I think you're going to have to take a long hard look at why that is. If you can't even be practical enough to set up a meaningful price structure, how can you hope to succeed?"

Clem felt the sting of his criticism and gritted her teeth. Uncle Jess's shop, which was now hers, was her pride and joy. How dare he imply that she wasn't a good businesswoman just because she refused to follow a rigid set of rules? She opened her mouth to tell him off when she remembered her motivation for this camping trip—to convince Will to make her a loan. This little exchange hadn't exactly scored any points for her, but she couldn't give up. Maybe she should try harder to answer his original question.

"Okay. Let's say I polished the stone and put it into

a silver tie tack setting and it turned out really pretty," she began, trying to sound pleasant.

"Now we're getting somewhere," Will said hopefully, rubbing his hands together.

"I'd maybe charge twenty-five."

Will looked as if he hadn't heard her correctly. "Twenty-five?"

"Twenty-five," Clem confirmed.

"Dollars?"

"What else?"

"You mean people spend their vacations here looking for rocks that are only worth a few dollars? I thought you said you could find a sapphire or ruby that could practically let you retire."

"A rock like that would be very rare," Clem explained. "Rocks like the one you just found are easier to come by. People enjoy finding rocks like that and having them put in inexpensive settings. It makes them happy to wear a stone that they found themselves. They don't care that it's not the Hope Diamond."

"You mean people actually pay good money and slog through the mud all day for *that*?"

Clem had to fight back her anger again when Will gave her a look that most people would reserve for the village idiot. She wouldn't stand idly by while he insulted her occupation and her favorite pastime. "Don't you understand? The joy is in the hunt."

When Will didn't respond, Clem threw up her hands in exasperation and rolled her eyes. "I'll bet you don't like to fish, either."

As a matter of fact, he didn't, but Will wasn't about to admit it after hearing the note of disgust in her voice. It seemed an unmanly admission to make to a woman who'd just led him into the wilderness, pitched two tents in ten minutes flat, and who could probably fend off wild animals with a wave of her hand.

Will watched as she jumped nimbly from rock to rock, moving upstream to the place where she'd set out some fish traps earlier. She was wrong about one thing. He did understand about the joy of the hunt.

What would it take to reel you in, my darling Clementine?

FOUR

In the early evening when the setting sun began to paint the sky in shades of orange and pink, Will leaned against a rock, watching Clem prepare a dinner of fried trout and baked potatoes. He thought about her earlier remark about fishing. Not that it was that much of a barb, really, but it did make him wonder if his lack of survival skills made her think him less of a man. Right now, she was ignoring him for all she was worth, and doing a helluva job at it.

Ruby lay down beside him and thumped her tail against the ground as he stroked her silky head. "Good girl," he murmured, wishing all females were as easy to please.

In his world, he didn't have to work to gain a woman's attention or approval. His reputation always preceded him. Women always came interested—automatically—like his laundry came neatly folded from the cleaners. Someone at a cocktail party would say, "I'd like you to meet Jane Doe. Jane, may I present Will Fletcher?" "Jane's" eyes would invariably widen, and her lashes would flutter. *"The* Will Fletcher?" She'd coo as her well-manicured hand lightly touched her throat in a gesture of nervous anticipation.

Meeting Clem was an eye-opener. When he'd admitted a little while ago that he'd never cleaned fish, he could have sworn she'd almost sneered at him. He wondered what it would take to impress a woman like her. Certainly not his business expertise. What little he'd shared with her earlier only seemed to annoy her.

So what *would* it take? What was that line in the old song about Davy Crockett—killed a bear when he was only three? "Three?" he could imagine her saying, "I was only *two.*"

Will closed his eyes, imagining a scenario in which Clem would visit him in Manhattan. He would take her to the floor of the New York Stock Exchange, to the top of the World Trade Center, to his high-rise apartment facing Central Park. Yes, he'd impress her all right. Then he'd take her to his bed.

"You must be having a nice dream."

"Huh?" Will opened his eyes to see Clem standing over him with a plate of steaming fish in her hand.

"If you died like that, it would take six undertakers to wipe that smile off your face."

"Only six?" Will sat up and took the plate from Clem, who returned to the fire to get her own food.

"Admit it. You're having a good time."

"No doubt about it." Will took a deep breath, savoring the aroma of the trout. She'd even made fritters from the cornmeal she'd used to batter the fish. He took a bite; it was delicious. "This sure beats freeze-dried Stroganoff. My compliments to the chef."

Clem laughed as she removed some fish from the bone and put it on a plate for Ruby. "Thanks."

Will hadn't realized how ravenous he was. Two fish

and several fritters later, he said, "So what's for dessert?"

Clem reached in her bag of provisions and pulled out a small plastic bag. "Marshmallows."

"What else?"

Clem got two sticks from a nearby sapling and sharpened one end on each of them with a dangerous-looking knife.

"I used to love to do this," Will said, securing a marshmallow to the end of the stick. "I was pretty good at it, too. I could get it perfectly done on both sides. In fact, I was the champion marshmallow roaster of my troop."

Clem started to do the same and paused. "So you were a Boy Scout? Somehow I can't picture that. I thought you said you never went camping."

"No, you assumed that. As a matter of fact, I went on several Scout camping trips."

"I'll be darned." Clem poked the fluffy candy onto her stick and held it out toward the flames. "What did you get your merit badges in? Let me guess. World economics? Finance, maybe?"

"Very funny. I'll have you know I had some very useful outdoor skills. I just seem to have forgotten them, that's all."

"My, but you are a risk-taker," she said as she removed a toasted marshmallow from the stick.

Will watched her as she carefully removed the candy, pursed her lips, and blew on it.

Heat surged through his body, and he knew it wasn't from the campfire. "I like to live dangerously." He leaned forward to kiss her, to taste the candy on her lips.

"Watch out!"

Will drew back the stick just in time to keep from

losing his marshmallow, which had blackened completely on one side. He saw Clem's skeptical look. "Just the way I like them." He ate the tarry marshmallow and said, "Now, where was I?"

"About to go back on your promise to behave like a perfect gentleman, I believe." Clem rose quickly and gathered up the dirty dishes.

As he watched her wash the dishes in a pot full of sudsy water, Will asked himself what had possessed him to make such a silly promise. Still, he supposed he could see why she'd be skittish alone in the woods with a man she hardly knew. He wanted her to like him and trust him. He was surprised by how important that felt to him. It had been a long time since a woman had so thoroughly fascinated him.

"I dreamed about a giant marshmallow the other night," he said.

"Don't tell me. You woke up and your pillow was gone."

"How'd you know?"

The sound of her laughter both relaxed and excited him. In a few minutes she joined him by the fire again. It was completely dark now, and the chirping, rustling, night sounds were beginning. "Isn't this where you get out your harmonica and play *'Red River Valley?'* " Will asked, breaking a twig and throwing it into the flames.

Clem smirked. "That's in the deluxe package. Costs extra."

"Well then, the least you can do is tell me another story." Will stretched out on his side.

"Okay," Clem agreed. She rolled her eyes toward the stars, as if trying hard to think of a good tale. "I've got it. There was this couple on a date, see?

And they ran out of gas just when this crazed guy with a hook for an arm was—"

"Not *that* kind of story," Will interrupted with a scolding look. "You don't want us to have nightmares, do you? I want a story like the ones you were telling this afternoon. What makes you such a good storyteller, anyway?"

Clem drew up one knee and wrapped her arms around it. "I guess it's because of my ancestry," she said thoughtfully. "I'm Scottish on my mother's side and Cherokee on my father's side. So I come from a storytelling tradition. Would you like to hear an Indian story?"

"By all means."

Clem positioned herself so that she sat directly across from Will, the fire between them, a little to one side of the closed front flap of one of the tents. Then, without a word, she put her long, slender, artist's hands together, and there sprang to life the shadow image of a bird in flight, projected perfectly onto the tent.

The shadow bird soared and dipped, plunging joyously through the make-believe sky. Will was amazed. He wanted to ask her where she'd learned this remarkable trick, but didn't want to break the spell she was weaving. When she began to speak, the sound was like music as ancient as time.

"There once was a beautiful bird," she began as the bird glided higher, frolicking in the air. "Its feathers were the brightest and most colorful of any bird's in the world. Redder than the berries, greener than the grass, and more yellow than the sun."

The bird glided lazily on a gentle current of air.

"Everyone loved the beautiful bird, but none so much as a certain brave young warrior. He was the son of the chief, and so he was rich. He had many ponies, and anything else that he wanted, except one thing. He wanted the beautiful bird for his own. So he built a cage from reeds and set out to trap her.''

The bird landed, preening herself with her dainty beak. Suddenly she gave a start. She fluttered frantically, darting from corner to corner of an imaginary cage, before coming to rest and hanging her tiny head.

"The warrior rejoiced that the bird was now his, but his joy soon turned to sorrow as the bird refused food and drink and grew weak and sick. Her feathers lost their luster, and she no longer sang her sweet song." The bird tucked her head under her wing, and was still.

Will turned his attention to the storyteller. The firelight bathed her in its golden glow and turned her hair to molten copper. Her silhouette, outlined on the tent, was like a separate being—as if the ghost of an Indian maiden had returned to help Clem tell the ancient tale.

"The warrior was inconsolable. He said a prayer to the Great Spirit, who said to him, 'Set her free and she shall sing once more. If you refuse, her cage will be her tomb.'

"The warrior went directly and did what he was told. Even though the bird would no longer be his, he released her to save her life."

Ever so slowly, the little bird began to flex, then flutter, her wings. Looking skyward, she took off, soaring higher and higher until she almost disappeared.

"The warrior was happy as he watched her, but sad as well, for she was gone. Then a strange thing happened. The bird swooped back toward the earth and landed on the warrior's shoulder. He was filled with joy because he knew that she would be with him always. She filled his life with beauty and song for all the days of his life."

Clem looked at Will expectantly.

Will exhaled, as if he'd been holding his breath a long time. "Wow," he said finally. "Where did you learn to do that?"

"From an aunt." Clem waved her hand as though it were nothing. "On the Cherokee side."

"That was the most impressive piece of performance art I've ever seen."

"Performance art?"

Will sat up and stretched. "That's where artists get a bunch of people together and . . . do lots of different things." He seemed at a loss for words.

"What kinds of things?"

Will scratched his head. "I don't know. Usually, things that have never been done before."

"Is that what makes something art? Just because it's never been done before?"

"I think that's what a lot of artists think. I once heard of a performance artist who drove a nineteen fifty-five Thunderbird into a lake to demonstrate the evils of materialism."

Clem was incredulous. "That's the dumbest thing I ever heard." "I thought it was pretty dumb, too." Will shook his head sadly. "That car was worth a fortune."

"Do they ever tell stories?"

"I'm not sure. Maybe sometimes," he said, smiling. "The point is, you created a whole other world with your words and your hands. It's spellbinding. You should go on the stage."

Clem smiled tolerantly at him, as if humoring a doddering fool.

"People would pay money to see you do that," Will persisted.

Clem shook her head. "I could never charge money for that. The old stories belong to everyone. I don't own them, so I certainly couldn't sell them."

Will sighed. "You're not much of a capitalist, are you?"

"You're paying for this trip, aren't you?" she shot back, smirking.

"True enough. But if you're going to turn your uncle's store around . . ."

Clem held up her hand. "It's getting late for shop talk. Let's call it a day."

Will agreed. Either Clem's story had mesmerized him to the point of near-unconsciousness or the hiking and prospecting had worn him out—either way, he couldn't keep his eyes open. "I'll tell you what," he said, climbing into his tent. "Let's sleep in tomorrow."

Clem doused the fire and threw dirt on the coals. "You're the boss." She got into her tent and slipped into her sleeping bag, the top of which stuck outside the tent slightly.

"Aren't you going to close the flap?" Will asked.

"In a while. I like to look at the stars first."

Will followed Clem's example, and looked up at the night sky. The fire was out, and with no other lights for miles the sky was alive with thousands of winking stars. He had never seen the stars more vivid.

He found himself wondering absurdly if Clem were responsible for this, too. Surely the stars had never been this brilliant before. After the day's events, he would have believed that she could do anything. Anything at all.

Clem turned her head to look at Will, and by the

light of the moon she saw the rapt smile on his face. He *was* having a good time. She was sure of it. As his lips parted slightly, she wondered what his kiss would have been like if she hadn't stopped him earlier. Would it have been tender, or demanding? Sweet, or sinful? Both? Just why had she stopped him, anyway? She was sure there must have been a reason, but looking at his perfect profile she couldn't think of one.

Even as she thought of his kisses, though, something nagged at her. It was what he'd said about charging money for the stories.

"Can you see the stars in New York City, or are the lights too bright?"

Will blinked and then opened his mouth as if to speak, but didn't for a while. "It's funny," he said, "I honestly don't know. I don't remember the last time I looked for them."

Clem sighed, genuinely saddened for this man who was rich by most standards but never thought to look to the stars.

Faster. Faster. Faster! The rabbit ran through the undergrowth, twigs and briars raking her fur. Darkness ahead, only darkness. Her tiny heart pumped hard enough to burst, but still she ran blindly. She could hear the fox behind her, feel its pursuit in the vibration of the spongy earth beneath her feet. It was getting closer. She could feel its breath now, heard it smacking its greedy mouth.

Clem woke with a start to feel Ruby's tongue licking her cheek. She couldn't see a thing but the dog's massive, fuzzy head. "Go on, you big fuzzball," she said, pushing Ruby away gently. "When I want a wake-up kiss from the likes of you, I'll ask for it."

When the dog moved out of the way, another face loomed above her, a much more pleasing one.

"Don't blame the dog. You were the one who woke *us* up in the middle of the night."

Will's eyes were heavy from sleep. With tousled hair and the beginnings of tomorrow's beard, he looked incredibly sexy.

"What were you dreaming about, anyway? You were moaning, and you looked as if you were trying to fight your way out of your sleeping bag."

Clem noticed for the first time that she was bathed in perspiration. Her heart was still beating rapidly, whether from the nightmare or the nearness of Will Fletcher, she couldn't say. "It was a nightmare. I was a rabbit, and a fox was after me."

Will stared at her thoughtfully. "I've never heard of that."

"What? You've never had a nightmare?" Clem rubbed her face.

"No. I mean having a nightmare from the point of view of an animal. That's really remarkable."

"Haven't you ever dreamt you were an animal?"

"No. And I've never heard of anyone else doing it until now." Will scratched his stubbly chin. "Are you always a rabbit?"

"Not always." Will began to stroke her hair gently. His touch electrified her. Her nerves were already jangly from her flight episode in the nightmare. Now they were positively raw. "Sometimes I'm other animals. Usually, I'm caught in a trap of some kind."

"That's awful." Will looked sincerely sympathetic. "Have you seen anybody?"

"Like who?"

"You know. A therapist."

"A shrink? Just for a few nightmares?" She might

plead guilty to being a country bumpkin, but she wasn't crazy.

"I know people who are in therapy for a lot less," he assured her. "I'll tell you what. I'll be your therapist. Tell me what you think causes these entrapment dreams."

"Talking about this stuff is really supposed to help you?"

"That's what they say."

Clem was skeptical. She loved talking about her early childhood in the mountains with her doting if eccentric relatives, her animals, and the outdoors, but she didn't like talking about the part of her past from which the nightmares sprang. Still, what could it hurt? Her edginess was responding nicely to his gentle scalp massage. She was feeling positively mellow, and in a more open frame of mind. She took a deep breath.

"I grew up in the cabin that I live in now. My dad was a lapidary like me, and a master silversmith. He taught me most of what I know. He and Uncle Jess worked out of the same shop I work in now. The shop didn't bring in enough money to support two families, so my dad worked the night shift in a mill in the next county." Clem swallowed hard. The next part was difficult, but Will didn't rush her. He just looked at her intently, with eyes as deep and dark as the surrounding forest.

"He died in an accident at the mill when I was twelve." Clem didn't meet Will's eyes. She hated pity of any kind. "A couple of years after that, my mother remarried. My stepfather is a construction worker, and has to go where the work is. So we wound up living in a tiny apartment in Pittsburgh. I guess it was a pretty tough neighborhood, because my mother wouldn't even let me go to the park."

Clem's throat constricted. She could almost feel the claustrophobia, the heat, the desperation. "As you can imagine, it was quite an adjustment for a kid who had grown up as wild and free as I had."

"I'm sure you were miserable," Will said, his brows drawing together in a pained look, as if he could feel what she felt.

She sighed. "It was like I was in prison. The spirit went clean out of me. I had always loved to draw, but I couldn't anymore. The creativity was gone. And of course I couldn't have any animals. And then there were the other kids."

"What do you mean?" he asked softly.

Clem paused again and took a deep breath. "Well, I talked differently, you know. Acted differently, I guess. The kids were pretty mean—called me names, beat me up, that sort of thing."

Will closed his eyes for a moment. When he opened them, she saw the pity and looked away. "What did you do? How did you get back here?"

"I begged constantly to go back home and visit Uncle Jess and the rest of my family. The year I was sixteen they bought me a bus ticket and said I could spend the summer in the mountains. When August rolled around, I was supposed to come back to the city in time for school."

"And you refused."

"That's right," Clem said. "They came to get me, but I was prepared."

"What'd you do?" Will leaned closer as if to see her better in the near darkness.

"I had gathered provisions all summer and stashed them different places in the woods—stuff that would keep, you know? Like dried fruit and meat, nuts, raisins, a few canned goods. That sort of thing. Then, when the time came, I just hid out. Remember that little glade I showed you when we first started out on the trail?"

"Yes. You said it was one of your favorite places."

"That's one of the places I lived. I pitched a little tent by the stream."

"Wow," Will said, clearly impressed. "How long did you hide?"

"Couple of weeks. It was easy. Since it was still summer, I never had to build any fires, so there was no smoke to give me away."

"Didn't they send someone to find you? Organize a search party or something?"

Clem shrugged. "No. All the neighbors knew the situation. I wasn't in any real danger. They also knew that nobody, with the exception of some of the Old Ones, knows the woods like I do."

"Sounds like a Mexican standoff. And let me just guess who blinked."

Clem allowed herself a smug smile. "They left word with Jess that they would let me stay as long as I agreed to enroll in high school here and get my diploma, which I did. I was watching the cabin the whole time, so I came out right after they left."

"Stealthy little devil, aren't you?" Will's eyes twinkled.

"I *am* part Indian, you know." Clem sniffed. "Anyway, I swore I'd never go to the city again, and I never will. The cabin had been in my dad's family, so I always had a place to live."

"So you've been totally on your own ever since." It was a statement rather than a question.

"I do have a pretty large extended family—aunts, uncles, cousins . . ." Clem stifled a yawn.

Will looked at her with sincere admiration. He'd known a lot of strong-willed women in his life, but this one took the cake. He *loved* strong-willed women. As strong as she was, though, she still had her demons, and they haunted her. In the silken darkness, she looked soft and vulnerable. She'd closed her eyes now, and her rhythmic breathing told him she was asleep. What a contrast she was—part tough, independent woman, part scared little girl, all in a wildly attractive package.

God, he wanted her. He now realized that his restlessness, his ennui, was not a case of burnout, after all. It was a yearning for something, and now that something had a name—Clementine. He was incredibly stimulated by both sides of her nature. The survivalist superwoman side challenged him, kept him on his toes. The childlike side made him want to vanquish her demons and protect her from harm.

There was so much he could give her. So much he could teach her. Not that he was into some *My Fair Lady* fantasy. He would never want to change her spirit, whatever gave her the passion for life that made her so exciting. To take this girl back to New York with him, though, turn her into a sophisticated woman—now, that would be a real challenge, just the kind of challenge he'd been looking for.

His earlier daydream of taking her to New York became more vivid, taking shape in his mind. Maybe he could make it happen.

There was a major obstacle. She hated the city. My God, living in a city was so traumatic for her that she still had nightmares about it. He'd think of a solution to that. He just had to. He'd also have to tread lightly.

His instinct told him that if he made any fast moves she would turn skittish on him and dance away, just out of his reach, as she had earlier.

He bent over her and kissed her forehead lightly. "Good night, wild child," he whispered. "Dream about me this time."

Will returned to his own tent. He fell into a fitful sleep and dreamed of caged birds and trapped rabbits.

Clem awoke with the dawn as usual, rising and stretching. She took several minutes to admire the sunrise as it stretched its orange and pink fingers over the mountains to the east. Since her experiences as an adolescent, she'd never taken her surroundings for granted, but revelled in the beauty of nature, whether it was a sunset, a babbling stream, or just a leaf. The mountains were her reason for living.

After taking a brief walk, she got her sketchpad out of her pack and sat cross-legged outside her tent. She remembered Will's intention to sleep late, and by the looks of him he would be dead to the world for quite a while, yet. That was fine with her. She liked time to herself, and besides, she felt particularly creative this morning.

She looked around her for something to sketch. There was that magnificent sunrise, of course, and the stream, the waterfall, but her gaze kept returning to the most inspiring sight in her line of vision—the sleeping face of Will Fletcher. His hair and brows were as black as night, and his skin was tanned. He had high cheekbones and a generous, sensual mouth. His tousled hair and the beginnings of a beard made him look a little wild, a little dangerous.

He no longer looked like the yuppie on holiday that he had just yesterday.

Clem began to sketch, letting her imagination run free. She drew him in the guise of an Indian warrior—powerful, strong, noble. The drawing was finished in minutes, and when she was through she held the pad out in front of her. Not bad.

He continued to sleep soundly. Clem fought the urge to stretch out beside him, unzip that sleeping bag, and let her fingers wander through that thick thatch of chest hair she'd glimpsed yesterday morning. "What you need is a cold shower, girl," she whispered to herself. She crawled back to her tent, removed a towel from her pack, and tiptoed past Will. He'd probably sleep for a couple more hours, she figured. Ruby was evidently on one of the early morning excursions she seemed to like so much.

When she reached the waterfall, Clem climbed up some rocks until she was well above the stream. She pressed her back to the cliff itself, which allowed her to squeeze behind the cascading wall of water to the far edge of the fall. There, a separate outcropping of rock above her head created a smaller waterfall, behind the main fall. It was a perfect natural shower, one she had used before.

Tossing her clothing onto a nearby bush, she steeled herself for the cold water. Closing her eyes, she stepped in, and had to suppress a yelp from the shock of the water, which felt cold enough to freeze into one gigantic icicle and trap her in it. It was exhilarating.

Will woke up slowly. One breath of the crisp mountain air and he knew before he opened his eyes that he wasn't in his bed in his Upper West Side apartment. Nope, this was different. He blinked and got an eyeful of early summer sun. He unzipped his sleeping bag and freed himself, stretching his long legs. Finally, he sat up and took in his surroundings, which he immediately noticed did not include his guide.

As he raked both hands through his hair to try to smooth down the wavy mass, Ruby loped into camp alone. "Where's Clem?" Will asked the dog, who trotted up to him, wagging her tail. Will gave her head a good scratching and was rewarded by a lick on the cheek. "I wish your mistress was as fond of kissing as you are," he remarked. "Now, where is she?"

Ruby stopped panting, reeling her generous tongue back into her mouth. This alone gave her a more serious look, but then she cocked her head to one side and fixed an expression on Will which was downright thoughtful. "Well?" he asked expectantly. She turned around and began to trot in the direction of the waterfall.

Will scrambled to put on his shoes. "Wait up!" He caught up with her at the stream and followed as she picked her way through the rocks. After a couple of minutes she stopped as if to allow him to catch up with her, but when he reached her side she remained seated on a large boulder and gazed serenely at the waterfall.

"Taking me sightseeing, are you? Well, listen, I really appreciate it, but I'm kind of busy right now." Something about the waterfall had caught Will's eye. He blinked, rubbed his eyes, and blinked again. He'd heard of mirages—in the desert—but they were not a phenomenon he'd ever associated with the mountains.

Maybe all the talk of dreams the night before had led him to have a particularly vivid one, and this was it. Or maybe he had simply taken leave of his senses. For whatever reason, he could have sworn that he saw Clem *inside* the waterfall. She was as naked as the day she was born.

FIVE

Will sat down so heavily on the rock that he almost bit his tongue. His mouth had been hanging open, and with good reason. He squinted into the morning sun and decided that he wasn't dreaming, after all. He wasn't sure exactly what he was seeing, but he knew one thing—he had to get a better look.

He made his way up and over several more large rocks and then paused when he came to a boulder almost as high as he was tall. Leaning against it with both hands, he peered over the top. His breath caught in his throat.

She wasn't inside the waterfall. She was behind it. At that angle, the wall of water was little more than a curtain, and a flimsy one, at that. Will allowed himself to exhale as his gaze devoured her from the top of her head to her slender feet—and everything in between.

He felt like a voyeur, invading her privacy like this. His mind told him he should leave, but the rest of him knew he wasn't going anywhere. She was exquisite—like some Indian water goddess, if there was such a thing. He remembered the perfect feminine form of the dragonfly fairy she had created for a piece of jewelry. He'd wondered at the time if it were a self-portrait. The answer was yes.

She had her arms drawn up across her chest, a defensive gesture against the onslaught of water. Then she dropped them to her sides and turned slightly, giving him an unobstructed view of her breasts, their rosy tips erect from the cold and from the not-so-gentle beating of the incessant water.

He heard himself groan, and tightened his grip on the rock as if it were his only hold on restraint.

Ruby joined him. She looked back and forth from Will to Clem and then let loose a healthy bark. "Hush!" he hissed. "You're going to give me away!" She barked again, reprovingly, he thought. "Whose side are you on?" As if to answer that question, she barked a third time, even louder.

Will bent down and cupped Ruby's head with his hands. "Shut up and I'll buy you a steak dinner. Just take it easy. I'm not going to hurt her." The dog shook herself free and darted around the boulder to the other side.

When Will stood up again, Clem was gone. "Damn!" he swore under his breath. She had undoubtedly heard the dog and run for cover. She'd might've even seen him, too. She was probably getting dressed in the stand of trees and bushes just beyond the other side of the falls.

Perhaps it was just as well she'd gone. One more minute, and he would have stripped naked and joined her. Then she would have run away and left him in the woods to fend for himself. He could see it now—*Investment banker eaten by bears. Film at eleven.*

Movement caught his eye downstream. Sure enough, Clem had stepped out of the undergrowth fully clothed, her hair wrapped in a towel. She went to where the stream narrowed and crossed it, so that she was back on the side where camp was.

Will sauntered back to camp as if returning from a leisurely morning stroll. Ruby was there, too, seated in front of where Clem was starting to rebuild the fire. The dog gave him what he could have sworn was a smug look and thumped her tail against the ground.

"I'm fixing us some pancakes for breakfast," Clem said without looking up. "I thought you'd still be asleep. Been up long?"

Will put his hands in his pockets and considered the question. Should he tell a gentlemanly lie and spare her embarrassment, or should he tell her the truth? After a moment he decided to split the difference and let her guess. "Long enough," he said cryptically.

As she stirred together pancake mix and water, Will noticed a slight hesitation in her movements. Then he added, "I always find a morning walk so . . . stimulating. So much so that I think I should go and take a cold shower while you're doing that. And I think I know just where to get one."

Although she kept her head down so that all he could see was a bit of her cheek, he definitely noticed a crimson streak showing up nicely next to the white towel. "I'll be right back," he said, strolling away toward the waterfall.

Oh, well. Nobody had ever accused him of being a gentleman, anyway.

When Will returned to eat breakfast, Clem used the activity of breaking camp to avoid looking at him, but she did force herself to keep up a conversation

as if nothing was wrong. He'd made it clear he'd seen
her taking a shower this morning. She wasn't sure
who she was more annoyed with—herself for being
stupid enough to be seen naked, or him for being
rude enough to admit he'd seen her. To make matters worse, he was so damned glib about it. He was
altogether the most exasperating man she'd ever
met!

It had been all she could do to keep from hiding
behind a rock and watching *him* naked. She remembered yesterday morning's pillow incident, and the
temptation was great, but she decided not to stoop
to his level.

As they got back onto the hiking trail, she managed
to keep up a more or less constant chatter about local
flora and fauna. To his credit, he at least pretended
to be interested, punctuating her speeches with
thoughtful questions. He seemed to be going out of
his way to put her at ease after teasing her earlier.
This softened her annoyance with him to the point
where she could actually look at him from time to
time.

Since he was roughing it, as he put it, he hadn't
shaved, so he had taken on a slightly swarthy look
that Clem found quite appealing. "You're looking
less like an investment banker and more like an outdoorsman," she observed.

"Thanks," Will said, looking pleased. "I think. By
the way, what's the next item on our itinerary?"

Clem nodded her head in the direction they were
going. "Up around the next big bend in the trail,
we're going to be crossing the road that leads into
the valley. There's a general store there that caters
to backpackers. We'll take on some more provisions
and check in with the owner. Uncle Jess will call him

later in the afternoon to make sure we arrived there sometime this morning."

"You think of everything, don't you?" He turned his glorious blue eyes on her with an appreciative look.

"I try," she said simply, her insides doing flip-flops. The trip was going well so far, she thought, resisting the urge to reach out and rap her knuckles on a tree trunk for superstition's sake. He was clearly impressed with her—she could tell. That made her happy, and not just because it helped her case for a loan. She was happy because *he* thought she was capable. How silly it seemed for one man's opinion to mean so much to her—*she* knew she was good at what she did. For some reason, though, when he looked at her in that admiring way—well, she could barely keep her knees from going to jelly.

They rounded the bend in the trail and came out into the clearing across the road from the store. As they crossed the road, Clem noticed three or four cars in the small parking lot. Against one of the cars, one with rental plates, reclined a woman in a smart linen pantsuit. It struck Clem that the woman looked like she was posing, like a model at an auto show. In fact, the woman could be a model. She was very slender, and taller even than Clem's five-foot-seven.

She was an altogether striking woman, Clem thought as she became aware that Will was making a beeline for her. As Will approached the woman, Clem became vaguely uneasy.

"My, but don't you look the ruffian?" the woman said in a low, languid, Lauren Bacall voice.

"Funny. You're the second woman to tell me that today. Judith, this is Clementine Harper, my wilderness guide. Clem, this is Judith Abernathy, one of my associates at the investment firm."

Judith turned to look at Clem as if she had only just noticed her. "Clem-en-tine." The woman spoke her name in a mock Southern drawl, all syrupy and drawn-out like in a bad sitcom. "How *precious!*"

Clem unclenched her teeth long enough to grind out, "Nice to meet you." Usually before people made fun of the way she talked, they waited until she had actually said something.

The woman was impeccably made up, her lip liner a tasteful shade darker than her lipstick and painted just outside the lipline for a more pouty, voluptuous look. It occurred to Clem that the same effect could be achieved by a good right hook to the mouth, something that she might just be able to arrange—especially if Judith continued to look at her as if she were a new and not entirely wholesome species of mammal that should be shooed back into the woods where it belonged.

"What are you doing here?" Will asked.

Judith fluttered her lacquered lashes and said coquettishly, "Surprised?"

"Nothing you do surprises me anymore, Judith."

Judith smiled broadly, evidently taking this as a compliment. It didn't sound like one to Clem.

"I brought you a modem to replace the one that mysteriously disappeared."

Clem looked at the ground to avoid Will's gaze, which she sensed was on her, and coughed.

"Ginger could just have air expressed me one. There has to be more to it."

"There is!" Judith said, clasping her hands together. "It's the Carter account. We've gotten word that McCarty Industries is planning a hostile takeover. You've got to put the plans in motion for a poison pill or some other device to stop the takeover."

Apparently, Judith's obvious enthusiasm wasn't shared by Will. Looking somewhat annoyed, he asked Judith a number of questions. Her responses were full of facts and figures. Clem, who didn't understand the questions or the answers, felt her earlier self-confidence ebbing. The trip had been going so well, and now it was over. Instead of spending that day and the next with her, Will would be working on a business deal with MBA Barbie.

Bitter disappointment washed over Clem, and it wasn't just because of the crimp the situation put in her plans for talking Will into the business loan. She liked being with him, and she didn't like the thought of losing his companionship to this woman.

Clem eyed Judith as the other woman continued her animated chatter. Judith reached out from time to time and touched Will's arm. There was an almost imperceptible possessiveness in her manner that made Clem wince.

"So, let's head to your cabin and get started, shall we?" Judith said as Will rubbed his chin. "I thought we'd start with—"

"No."

Judith smiled, and a look of relief passed over her perfect features. "Of course. This is not the kind of thing you want to handle long distance. We'll head for the airport immediately and send someone for your things."

"No," Will said again, in the same authoritative tone.

Judith looked at him blankly, as if she couldn't believe her ears. "What?"

"I'm on vacation, and I'm not cutting it short. The

Carters can wait until tomorrow afternoon when I get back. You can stay in the cabin until then if you want to, but you'd probably be of more use if you went back to the office and handled your end from there."

Clem was overjoyed. She felt herself beaming at Will, who gave her a slight wink. When she looked back at Judith, the woman was staring hard at her. Gone was the urgency she'd exhibited over the business dealings. She was back to the cool, impassive look she'd worn earlier. One corner of her mouth quirked upward in a half-smile as she looked Clem up and down, then Will.

Clem felt as if she could almost read Judith's thoughts as the other woman sized up the situation. She returned Judith's gaze evenly. She would not show any weakness toward an interloper in her territory—the animals had taught her that.

Judith suddenly turned a dazzling smile on Will. "I have a better idea. Since you seem to be having such a wonderful time, why don't I join you? I haven't had a real vacation in ages, as you know." Judith lowered her voice and leaned toward Clem. "He's a real slave driver. I canceled a European vacation last fall because of a merger we had to close."

Clem saw Will frown. How manipulative could you get? Judith had executed the guilt trip as smoothly as silk. She was good, Clem acknowledged grudgingly. No way was Will going to say no to her request to come along.

"Well, I guess—" Will began as Judith hopped over to him and put her slender arms around his neck.

"This is going to be so much *fun,*" she said effusively. "It can be like one of those team building trips. It'll add a new dimension to our relationship.

Besides, I've always wanted to do something . . . out-doorsy."

Clem crossed her arms, watching Judith's display with annoyance. She noted again Judith's perfect hair, nails, and makeup, the way her tailored pantsuit looked pristine even after a plane flight and long drive from the airport. Linen didn't wrinkle on this woman. How did she do it? However she did it, it was going to be a whole lot tougher doing it on a back-packing trip.

Will didn't extricate himself from Judith's embrace as quickly as Clem would have liked. When he did, he turned to Clem. "I've got to place a call to the office. Take Judith and gather up everything she'll need for the trip. I'll be along in a few minutes."

As they entered the store, Will asked Judith, "How'd you find us, anyway?"

"When I didn't find you in your cabin, I stopped at the nearest business—a jewelry store of some kind. An old geezer told me you'd gone on a camping trip, and that you'd be coming by here today before noon."

Will gave Clem an apologetic smile and excused himself to make the phone call. As Judith wandered off to examine some hiking boots, Clem greeted the owner, a jovial, bearded, bear of a man. "How goes it, Jim?"

"Not bad. Having a nice trip?"

"Well, we *were.*" Clem inclined her head toward Judith.

Lowering his voice, Jim said, "Your uncle Jess called and said to tell you that he's sorry he had to tell that woman where you and your client were. She insisted that she had to speak with him, and it sounded urgent."

"When he calls back, tell the 'old geezer' that I said I understand." Clem watched Judith poke gingerly at a package of trail mix as if the cellophane bag contained moon rocks instead of raisins and nuts.

"And he said something else," Jim whispered conspiratorially. "He said he got bad vibes from her."

"He ain't the only one, my friend," Clem confided. She left her pack with Jim and went to join Judith, who was checking her makeup in a compact mirror. She wore an expression of bored indifference that would have done any runway model proud.

"Let's get started, shall we?" Judith said, closing the compact with a snap.

"Good idea." Clem led the way to a display of backpacks and briefly explained the different types and the advantages of each. She was just about to make a recommendation when she got the distinct impression that Judith, although looking at her intently, hadn't heard a word she said.

"You know," Judith said, wagging a perfectly manicured finger at Clem, "you remind me of someone."

Clem sensed something unpleasant was on its way, and steeled herself. The long-suppressed feeling seemed as familiar as if she'd felt it just yesterday, and as painful. It sprang from the same collection of sensations she'd experienced whenever she was taunted at school so long ago—shame, rejection, isolation.

"Someone on television or in the movies," Judith continued with a don't-tell-me-let-me-guess look. "I think it's either Ellie Mae Clampett or . . . Tammy. That's it. I've just walked in on a scene from *Tammy and the Investment Banker*."

As Judith laughed heartily at her own joke, Clem's

fingers itched to reach for the cast-iron skillet on the shelf next to her left hand.

"Since I don't look anything like Sandra Dee, I can only assume that you're complimenting me on my folksy charm," Clem said evenly.

Judith gave her a contrite look. "Of course. Oh, my, did I insult you?"

"Not at all."

Judith picked up a backpack that Clem knew was the least comfortable and the most expensive. "I don't think you want that one."

"Oh, but it's a designer bag," Judith said, pointing to the fancy patch sewn on the front. "This logo means quality."

"Whatever you say."

Judith put on the backpack, but appeared stymied by the buckles. She seemed to be afraid of ruining her nail polish. While Judith plucked gingerly at the fastenings, Clem pointed her toward a rack of clothing. Clem left her to select her hiking outfit and returned to the counter.

Jim stroked his beard with one beefy hand. "You know," he said, grinning slyly, "a camping trip can be quite an ordeal for someone who's not mentally prepared. You could play some good tricks on her. The old snipe hunt is still a good one. I'd like to see this chick get left holding the bag."

"Not that the idea isn't tempting, but my client is paying me big bucks to keep him and his guest out of trouble, so that's what I'm going to do." Clem leaned her elbow on the counter and observed that Judith was already having trouble with the backpack, and it hadn't even been loaded yet. "If she gets herself in a jam, it'll be her own doing, not mine."

"I admire your professionalism." Jim returned her skeptical look with a smile. "Really. I mean it."

Judith stepped up to the counter with two hiking outfits and a spray can of bug repellant.

"Oh, you don't need that," Clem said. "I've got some homemade stuff that's better, if I can just find it." She took her first aid kit from her backpack and emptied the contents onto the counter. "Here it is," she said, reaching for a tiny bottle.

Not waiting for Clem, Judith grabbed a different bottle and opened it.

"Wait! That's—" Clem began, and stopped as Jim put a silencing hand on her arm.

"Just what you need," Jim finished.

Judith's nose wrinkled as she applied the greasy salve to her face and arms. Then she capped the bottle, pocketed it, and headed for the display of hiking boots.

"What were you thinking? She picked up Jess's fish lure potion by mistake. That's stuff's probably going to attract insects instead of repel them," hissed Clem.

Jim's laughter rumbled deep in his chest. "I know. Ain't it great?"

As Clem and the store owner debated the wisdom of telling Judith the truth about the bug repellant, Ruby sauntered in. Jim greeted her by name and she wagged her tail. Leaning on the counter, Clem caught a bit of motion out of the corner of her eye. Actually, it wasn't motion at all, but the sudden cessation of it. Judith had gone stock-still in the middle of tying a bootlace. She and Ruby stared at each other as if facing off for a duel.

Clem looked at her good-natured pet as the animal's upper lip curled in the beginnings of a snarl.

"I've never seen her hate anybody on sight like that," Clem said, astonished.

Jim inclined his head toward Judith. "Looks like the feeling's mutual."

As if on cue, Judith called out, "Do you allow dogs in here?"

"Yep," Jim answered simply.

Clem walked over to Ruby and stroked her head, calming her. "Ruby, I'd like you to meet Judith. Judith, this is my friend and our travelling companion, Ruby."

Judith worked her jaw a second before she spoke. "You don't mean to say that animal is coming with us?"

"Oh, yes," Clem said deliberately. "I do."

Judith had opened her mouth to speak again when Will walked up and stood on Ruby's other side. He gave the dog a couple of affectionate pats on the back. "I see you've met Ruby. Isn't she great?"

"She's a beauty." Judith managed a fetching smile.

After Judith brought the new boots to the counter, she produced a credit card to pay for it all. Jim rang up the merchandise, and Judith excused herself to change into her brand new hiking outfit.

Clem knelt in front of the counter and put the provisions into her and Will's packs while he loaded Judith's. "I hope you don't mind the change in plan," he said.

"Adaptability is my middle name," Clem assured him. His pack sat on the floor between them. As she reached to close it, Will covered her hand with his own.

"This isn't what I would've wanted. But Judith's been a good friend and a trusted associate."

And what else? Clem wanted to ask. Her eyes

searched his for an answer. She saw apology there, but nothing more. His touch was warm and reassuring.

"She's always been there for me," he continued.

"I understand." Clem gave him what she hoped was a reassuring smile even as she longed to know what they were to each other, besides good friends and associates. She would have bet her eyeteeth they'd been lovers. The looks Judith gave him practically shouted it. The knowledge gave her a sick feeling.

"You might find Judith a little . . ." Will paused, searching for the right word. "Aggressive. In the work she and I do, that's actually an advantage. Out here, it might seem a little abrasive."

No kidding.

By the time they had repacked, Judith joined them and they all went to her car. Clem noticed that she had rolled up the legs of her khaki hiking shorts to make them even shorter. Judith stored her neatly folded suit in the trunk and got some additional items from her suitcase to add to her pack. Clem shook her head when the woman stuffed a rather large makeup case into her pack. As Judith leaned far forward into the car's trunk, Clem noticed that the view of her derriére she presented was not going unnoticed by Will.

As they got onto the trail, Judith continued her earlier briefing about the business deal, then went on to other pending business and general news and gossip from the office. Although she didn't understand much of what was being said, Clem comforted herself with the knowledge that here in the woods it was her own talent, her own expertise, that they would be depending on. They were on her turf now.

As Judith droned on, Clem noticed Will wrinkling his nose whenever the woman leaned toward him, which was often. "Eau de Trout Lure" was working its special magic, Clem thought. It had been hard to stifle a giggle when Ruby, with her sensitive nose, had gotten a whiff of the stuff on Judith. Clem had never seen a dog actually gasp before.

"This conversation can't be much fun for Clem," Will said finally. "Let's save the rest of the shop talk for later and enjoy the hike."

Judith's smile held just the hint of a pout before she graciously turned her attention to Clem. "So, what do you do besides usher people through the woods?"

"I'm a lapidary."

"I've seen her work," Will said. "It's terrific. She's a very talented artist."

"An *artist*. Well, well, well." Judith's face became more animated at this piece of news, Clem noted. It seemed to please her. "This is fascinating."

"Why?" Clem sensed she would not like the answer.

Judith leaned toward Clem and gave her a predatory smile. "Because Will positively despises artists."

SIX

Will gave Judith a warning glance. "You seem to have forgotten one of my best friends is an artist."

"A dancer. That doesn't count," Judith insisted. "Actually, I think it's just the artists who come to him for financial help that get on his nerves."

Clem felt as if she'd received a blow to the solar plexus. With effort, she managed not to break stride. Great. In one fell swoop Judith had dashed her hopes for a business loan, confirmed that Will disliked artists, and then let slip that he had a "friend" who was a dancer—probably a leggy, gorgeous one, at that. Judith was just a wealth of glad tidings. Too bad shooting the messenger was out of style.

Clem remembered the first time she and Will had discussed art, and his later remarks about her business sense. It all fit together now. He really did have a problem with artists.

"What Judith is referring to is based on an incident that's ancient history," Will said, then deftly changed the subject. "Clem, why don't you explain to Judith what we'll be doing this afternoon?"

Clem did as she was told, disappointed that she was not to learn more about what was behind Will's feelings for artists—not yet, anyway. "We're going to a mine on a hill a few more miles from here, so you two can pan for sapphires. It belongs to a friend of mine, so I have his permission to use it. He said it was okay for us to camp there, too, which will be nice since the place has running water. The tourist season doesn't start for a couple more weeks yet."

"Tourist season?" Judith arched one eyebrow. "This place has a tourist season?"

"This is sapphire country," Clem explained patiently. "People come here from all over to look for sapphires and rubies on their vacations."

Judith glanced to Will for confirmation. Clem's word alone wasn't quite enough for such an unlikely tale.

"Although most of the stones people find are not very valuable, they still enjoy the thrill of the hunt. And they like to have lapidaries like Clem cut and polish the rocks and make them into inexpensive jewelry they can keep as mementos of their vacations." Will waited for Clem to express her approval of his successful summary of the speech she'd given him the day before.

"I couldn't have said it better myself," she said. Maybe he was beginning to understand, after all. Or maybe he was just humoring her.

Will gave her a smile so devastating that Clem felt as if she surely glowed from the reflection of it. She knew the warmth came from inside, though, from the feeling he was starting to give her every time she looked at him.

Judith must have sensed the special moment between the two. Her jaw became set in a hard line and her eyes flashed darkly, but she said nothing.

They made small talk for the rest of the hike. When they'd reached their destination they took off their packs, and Clem showed them where they would make camp. After they ate a leisurely lunch, Clem and Will pitched the two tents on a level spot of ground between the mine and another pleasantly babbling trout stream. Will volunteered to forage for wood to fuel that night's campfire, while Clem unpacked the tools and provisions. Judith took the opportunity to touch up her makeup.

Clem stowed Will's pack in his tent and put her and Judith's packs into her own. As Clem started to zip the tent, Judith appeared at her side.

"I'm sharing *Will's* tent," Judith said flatly. She gave Clem a poisonous smile.

Clem took a deep, calming breath. "Whatever," she said evenly. Gritting her teeth, she backed off from the tent opening, allowing Judith to remove her pack. Clem took the panning boxes and tools over to the flume as Judith donned a pair of designer sunglasses and applied more of the homemade "bug repellant."

Clem started to confess the true identity of the potion, then thought about Judith and Will spending the night in the close confines of the tent. "Nah," she drawled under her breath.

Clem got a bucket from the tiny shed near the flume and filled it with some of the earth that had been dug out of the mine. When Will returned, she demonstrated sapphire panning for Judith and explained what to look for. When Will showed Judith the sapphire he'd found the day before, Judith seemed duly impressed.

Clem climbed the hill and opened a large spigot, sending water down the flume. As she made her way down the hill to see how the panning was going, Judith began to shout. "My watch! It's gone. I've lost it in the flume." Frantically, she looked around her.

"Calm down, we'll find it," Will assured her.

Clem helped Will look for the watch, but apparently didn't exhibit enough urgency to suit Judith. "Don't just stand there. It's a *Cartier!*"

Clem pointed to the end of the flume. "It might have washed all the way out of the flume. You might want to look at where the water's running off down the hill. Maybe it's snagged on something."

Judith hurried down the hill. At the end of the flume was a large hole that collected the runoff water. She bent over it, trying in vain to see into the murky depths.

"She'll never find it in that mud," Will observed, shaking his head.

Clem saw Ruby approaching Judith in the stealthy crouch she usually reserved for flushing quail. "Ruby! No! Get away!"

Ruby issued an ardent bark from about a foot away from Judith's backside. Judith screamed and took an involuntary step forward, finding herself teetering on the edge of the mudhole. Her arms flailed in her effort to backpedal herself out of the inevitable. For a moment she looked like a Barbie doll doing a bizarre interpretive dance. Then she went in with an impressive splash.

Will and Clem hurried to reach her, slipping and sliding on the viscous mud. Clem knew that the hole was only about waist deep, but Judith evidently thought she was drowning. "I think you need to just put your feet on the ground," Clem offered.

After a few moments, Judith stopped flailing and screaming and did as she was told. Will offered his hand and she meekly took it, allowing him to haul her from the hole. Her brand new hiking outfit and boots were covered with reddish brown mud.

"Are you all right?" Will said, putting a hand on Judith's shoulder.

Judith sputtered something unintelligible, and something else that wasn't.

"Let me show you where to wash up and then we'll find your watch," Clem said, leading a trembling Judith toward the shed. While Judith cleaned up at a small sink inside, Clem brought her a change of clothes from Judith's pack. Clem then joined Will at the mudhole with the panning boxes and handed him one.

Will eyed her as he rolled up his sleeves. "I can't help but wonder."

"Hmm?" Clem reached into the hole with the panning box.

He got on his knees on the opposite side of the hole and looked into her face. "Correct me if I'm wrong, but I'm getting the impression that you and Judith aren't hitting it off too well."

"I've learned that it takes all kinds," Clem remarked philosophically.

Will paused, as if searching for the right words. "You were telling me yesterday about how you have a special rapport with animals. I was just wondering. . . ."

Clem didn't like the direction this was taking, and glared up at him.

He grinned sheepishly. "It was just a thought. Never mind."

Sheesh, Clem thought. Did he really think she would sic her dog on Judith just because she didn't like her? Clem looked up at Ruby, who sat nearby wearing her usual goofy doggie grin. Well, she certainly hadn't done it *consciously,* anyway.

Clem bent over and reached into the hole with the sieve box, finding that she could just reach the bottom with it. Her next attempt to snare the watch came up empty, but she tried again. Will did the same thing from his side of the hole. After a minute or so, they reached in at the same time and bumped heads. Laughing, Clem clutched her head, smearing mud on her face in the process.

Will laughed too, an easy, deep laugh. The manly music made Clem tingle from her head to her toes. She'd gladly get hit upside the head anytime if it meant she could hear that sound.

Will edged around to kneel beside Clem and took a bandanna from his pocket. He made a soothing sound that drew her to him as he dabbed the mud from her forehead. "Let me wipe off some of that warpaint, wild child," he murmured.

Clem looked up to see a very annoyed Judith standing beside them. "Well, have you found my watch?" she asked venomously.

Clem looked into the box she still held. "Why, yes. I believe I have." She rubbed the mud off the face of the watch and held it out to Judith with a triumphant smile.

Judith snatched the watch from Clem and stalked away.

Clem and Will spent the remainder of the afternoon pleasantly panning for sapphires in the flume while Judith sat by the campfire in stony silence. The silence was interrupted only once, when Ruby again startled Judith, this time while she was reapplying her makeup. Just as Judith was using her eyelash curler, the dog brought her a dead mouse as a peace offering.

"You know, I don't think Judith appreciated Ruby's gesture very much," Will said once Judith had calmed down again.

"I think you're right," Clem agreed. "Which is too bad. I mean, Ruby's intentions were good. And it's not like those eyelashes won't grow back."

Judith still acted a mite nervous at supper time, Clem noted as she dished up steaming helpings of the rice and sausage dish she'd prepared. Judith kept looking behind her, presumably so nothing could sneak up on her.

After the meal, Clem gathered the rest of the food into a nylon mesh bag, tied it with a rope, and tossed the rope over a nearby tree limb. She then pulled the rope so that the bag was seven or eight feet off the ground.

"Why are you doing that?" Judith asked, her eyes narrowing.

"This will keep the bears and raccoons away from the food." Clem tied the rope securely around the tree.

Judith leaped to her feet, balling both hands into fists. "You're absolutely insufferable!"

"What?" Clem braced herself—for what, she didn't know.

"You know exactly what I'm talking about," Judith insisted, looking to Will for support. Will only sat cross-legged, watching the two women expectantly as if waiting for some kind of performance to begin.

"You've tried to intimidate me since you first learned I was going on this camping trip," Judith continued, her dark eyes blazing. "You had your dog attack me, not once but twice! And now you're trying to frighten me into believing that we're in danger from bears. Well, you can just save your breath. I'm not falling for it. I don't believe there are any bears for miles."

As Clem listened to the other woman rant, she tried to determine if the outburst was sincere or if it was being staged for Will's benefit. Judith had managed to make herself look silly twice that day. What better way to salvage her image in Will's eyes than to blame the incidents on Clem? Well, she wasn't going to get away with it.

"If you believe there are no dangers in these woods, then you believe wrong," Clem said calmly and with as much authority as she could muster. "Will is paying me to lead the two of you on a camping expedition. And if I'm to return you to civilization intact, I strongly suggest you follow my instructions. If you have a problem with that, I'm afraid I can't be held responsible for your safety."

Judith's mouth formed a tight little "o" of silent indignation. Will's expression was serious, but otherwise unreadable. After a palpable pause, Will said, "Yes, ma'am."

"Ooh!" Judith stormed away toward Will's tent.

Clem shook her head in exasperation. The nerve of that woman.

"Is it true?" Will asked simply.

Clem could hardly believe her ears. She sat down across the campfire from him. He waited expectantly, not moving. His silhouette was framed by the setting sun, which crowned the distant ridges with fire and cast a golden aura around him. His hair shone blue-black, and his eyes reflected the light of the campfire, if not its warmth.

Clem returned Will's frank gaze. "Isn't it true that I warned you about bears on the first leg of this trip?"

"Yes."

"And isn't it true that I tied up the food in just the same way when we made camp last night?"

"Yes."

Clem held her head high. "And do you believe for one minute that I can actually make animals do tricks by . . . by telepathy or something?"

"I believe you could do anything." Although Will's mouth was set in a hard line, the sternness didn't reach his eyes, which twinkled mischievously.

"Well!" she gasped in indignation. "I don't know how to take that. Are you complimenting my way with animals, or are you saying that you think I'm capable of terrorizing someone just because I don't like her?"

"You don't like her? Why not?" Will lazily raised one brow.

She might have just made a tactical error, Clem acknowledged to herself, but to hell with it. "Don't change the subject."

"Very well. What I meant was, I've come to appreciate your many skills over the last couple of days. So much so that I would believe you could do almost anything if you put your mind to it."

Clem was silent for a moment. She felt the same rush of warmth she always did when he praised her. "Well, thanks. But I didn't sic Ruby on Judith. Those two took an instant dislike to each other."

"So why don't *you* like Judith?" A grin played at the corner of Will's mouth.

She wished he'd forgotten about that part. "Well, Ruby doesn't like her, and . . . and she's always been an excellent judge of character, so that's good enough for me. Besides, you said yourself that Judith's abrasive."

"Is that all it is?" Will raised an eyebrow.

Clem decided it was time to make her exit before she got herself in any deeper. "I'm too tired for this. I'm going to bed." The sound of his gentle laughter as she retreated sent tickling waves of pleasure down her spine.

Judith stared at the roof of the tent and then over at Will. How could he sleep so soundly with her right beside him? There was a time when he wouldn't have ignored her presence in his bed. Not that they were in bed, exactly. These damned sleeping bags didn't leave much room for cohabitation. Still, she had left hers unzipped when she'd turned in—hoping that he would be open to a little cuddling, at least—but when he crawled into the tent, he'd ignored her and zipped himself up like a moth in a cocoon. It was that little hillbilly's fault. She had bewitched him somehow.

Judith decided that she needed to find the old miner's outhouse Clem had pointed out to her earlier in the day. She unzipped her sleeping bag, put on her boots, and fumbled in her pack for her penlight.

Once outside the tent, she turned on the tiny light, which did little to illuminate the surrounding darkness. That hound from hell was probably lying in wait for her somewhere, but she'd be on her guard. She decided to train her light on the ground to avoid stepping on anything creepy and crawly. She set out in the direction of the outhouse without pausing for her eyes to adjust to take advantage of the moonlight.

She hadn't gone far when something rough-textured struck her on the side of the head. "What?" She pointed her light upward to see the bag of food swinging wildly right in front of her face. As the bag passed by like a giant pendulum, something else filled her line of vision. Something furry. And very, very large.

The still night air was shattered by bloodcurdling screams.

Disoriented from being rudely roused from a deep sleep, Clem unzipped the tent as quickly as she could, and she and Ruby burst out of the opening together. The moon was just bright enough now for her to see where she was going. She realized that the screams were taking her in the direction of the flume. If Judith was running blindly away from something, she would crash into the flume and break both legs. The sound of a loud splash came as a relief. She'd missed the flume, but she'd once again found the mudhole.

Judith thrashed about in the mudhole, wailing hysterically.

"Put your feet on the ground. You're not in over your head," Clem told her, to no avail. Shaking her head, Clem squatted down and slipped into the mudhole with Judith. Clem grasped the woman's shoulders and shook her, but this seemed only to convince Judith that Clem was trying to drown her. The frantic woman came at Clem with the strength that only a whopping surge of adrenaline could produce, slamming Clem against the far side of the hole.

"Good grief," Clem muttered as she staggered to her feet. She shoved Judith an arm's length away and slapped her smartly across the face. The wailing stopped at the same time that a bright flashlight beam blinded the two combatants.

"My goodness, what have we here?" Will stood

above them, training the beam of light on first one, then the other. "If you two were planning a mud wrestling match, you could at least have had the decency to let me watch."

The wisecracks continued as Will helped them up and out of the hole. "You know, you guys could go to Times Square and get paid for this."

Once back on solid ground, Clem turned to Judith. Her hair hung in muddy clumps and dirty leaves and twigs stuck to her clothing. Clem might have laughed if she hadn't known that she looked exactly the same. "What the hell happened?"

Judith hugged her arms and looked frantically all around her. "It was a b-b-bear. It was up on its hind legs trying to get the food, and then it came after me!" Her sexy alto had become decidedly shrill.

Clem pictured the scene of Judith coming face-to-face with a rearing bear. What she wouldn't have paid to see that! *"Now* do you believe I wasn't just trying to scare you by warning you about bears?"

An apparently contrite Judith nodded. She looked so pathetic that Clem almost felt sorry for her.

"Do you think it'll be back?" Judith asked weakly.

"No. I imagine you scared it out of its wits with your screaming, and since it didn't even get any food to show for its trouble I doubt it'll be back."

"Don't take this the wrong way, but you really need to get out of those wet clothes," Will said. "This springtime air is going to get colder and colder the longer you stand around dripping wet."

Will rebuilt the campfire as the women cleaned up and changed in the shed. Because of her earlier encounter with the mud, Judith had no dry clothes to change into, so Clem gave her the shorts and T-shirt she had planned to wear on the return trip. Clem would wrap up in a blanket, and hope her own clothes would be dry by morning.

Clem tied a length of rope between two trees. She then hung the clothes on the makeshift clothesline. After Judith had warmed herself sufficiently by the fire, she quietly excused herself and went back to bed.

"I've never seen her that quiet," Will observed after Judith was out of earshot. He was sitting across the fire from Clem.

Clem smiled. The blanket wrapped loosely around her, she returned to the fire and stood bending over it, hoping to dry her hair as much as possible. She looked up to see Will watching her. Even in the near darkness, she could see the unmistakable gleam in his eyes. "I wish I had shorter hair like Judith's. It would be dry by now."

"No," Will said hoarsely. "Don't say that. Your hair is beautiful."

Clem didn't look up, but continued spreading and separating her hair with her fingers. Still, she could feel his eyes on her as surely as she could feel the heat from the fire.

"Aren't you going to bed, too?"

"How could I possibly sleep after all this excitement?"

Clem dared a glance at him from the corner of her eye. She felt the color rise to her cheeks as his gaze travelled the length of her body. "Yes, it's not every day that a bear invades your campsite."

"*That* was certainly exciting, *too.*" he said. His wicked grin left no doubt as to his meaning.

The wind shifted, sending smoke in Clem's direction, so she moved to the other side of the fire to avoid it. Now she was between Will and the flames, not realizing that the effect allowed him to see her silhouette through the thin blanket.

Will drew in his breath and held it for a long while. He'd never wanted a woman more in his life. If not for Judith's presence just a few yards away, Clem would be in his arms right now.

Clem moved again to the other side of the fire, the smoke and flames reaching up to her. She looked for all the world like a beautiful phoenix rising from the ashes of some ancient fire, a mythical creature taking shape before his very eyes. She was charming him, bewitching him as he suspected she had the animals.

He thought of the bear he'd seen earlier as it ambled out of camp. It took Will a moment to find his voice. When he did, he said, "It was him, wasn't it?"

Clem pushed her veil of hair to one side and looked up at him, puzzled. "Who?"

"Your pet bear."

"Don't be silly. There are hundreds of black bears in these woods. What in the world makes you think that bear was my pet?"

Will paused to drink in the sight of her again. She was standing erect now, her hands on her hips, her chin thrust out, as if expecting another confrontation about her animal friends. "Tell me something," he finally began. "Is Ruby in the habit of approaching strange bears and licking them in the face?"

Will watched this news sink in. Clem's eyes grew round, and she blinked several times. Then her defensive expression returned. "As God is my witness," she said slowly, "I did not conjure up that bear to frighten anyone."

Will held his hands up in defeat. "I give. So you can't charm animals to do your will."

"I didn't say I can't." Clem smiled a smile full of

mystery, primal power, and perhaps even danger. "I said I didn't."

Her hair hung loosely about her shoulders and, wrapped in the colorful blanket she looked every bit the Indian princess that he was sure she had been in some ancient incarnation. Between the moonlight and the firelight, her whole image shimmered like a mirage before him—a mirage that would disappear if he reached out to touch her.

How he ached to reach out and touch her. But he couldn't. Not now. Not yet.

SEVEN

Will remained by the dying fire long after Clem had gone to her tent. He knew he wouldn't be able to sleep, haunted as he was by Clem's words and by how she'd looked in the firelight. He had never met a woman like Clem before. She was making him believe in possibilities he would have scoffed at just a few short days ago.

He stared into the embers, which were still glowing faintly, and breathed deeply of the woodsy aroma. He realized that the time he and Clem had together would be over tomorrow. He had to think of a way to keep her near him, and not just while he was here in the mountains. He had to get her to New York with him—get her away from the forest, streams, and campfires that were helping her bewitch him. On his turf, he could see if his attraction to her was real or just a temporary enchantment. With her aversion to the city, it would be a tough challenge. It was a good thing he loved a challenge.

Will's hands clutched at the ground, and his right hand closed around a twig. He reached out and put the twig on the coals and watched the tiny flame spring to life again.

* * *

"Judith's quiet this morning," Will observed after breakfast. They were repacking the tents as Judith sat near the remains of the campfire. Her straight-ahead stare was punctuated every now and then by a quick look over her shoulder.

Clem zipped her pack. "I'm afraid catatonic's more like it."

"I wonder how long she'll be in therapy over this." Will scratched his chin, which by now sported the beginnings of a beard as black as his hair.

"She'll probably be fine as soon as her feet hit Manhattan soil—or should I say pavement?"

Will chuckled. "You're probably right."

"Isn't it funny? She's terrified by this environment where I feel so at home, but if I were to go to New York where she feels safe, I'd be the catatonic one." Clem shook her head and shuddered.

Will's expression became serious for a moment and then he smiled again. "It's not so bad, you know. It has a bad rep, but it can be a great place. The art scene alone would be terrific for you."

Clem looked at him skeptically. She had started to reply when Judith called to them, "Can't we get on the trail now, please?"

Clem and Will shouldered their packs. "Just think about it." He squeezed her arm and walked over to join Judith. Clem looked after him, wondering what he'd meant. She absently ran her fingers over the place he'd touched.

Judith remained subdued on the trek back, perking up a little only when she was told that they were getting close to their final destination. At this point they were closer to Will's cabin than to the wilderness store, so they decided to remain on their original course and go back for Judith's rental car later. Judith was only too happy to take the shortest route back to civilization.

Clem stole a wistful look at Will. She reckoned that when he got back to the cabin, he'd probably shave. Too bad. The beard really suited him. It would be good-bye to Will the outdoorsman, and hello again to Will the investment banker. *That will probably suit Judith just fine,* thought Clem, annoyed.

The really depressing thought was that Will would be going back to New York soon, and what time he had left here would probably be spent with Judith in his cabin. That part bothered her most of all. What a fool she'd been to have allowed herself to think of him as anything more than a customer and potential source of credit. In the short time they'd spent together, he had become important to her, and she didn't form attachments easily. She couldn't bear to think that she might never see him again. He, on the other hand, seemed to be in terrific spirits, making jokes and tossing sticks to Ruby.

Clem sighed. While Judith seemed so preoccupied, and Will seemed in such a good mood, she guessed she might as well broach the subject of the loan. She might not get another opportunity.

"So how did you enjoy the trip?" she began.

"You have to ask?" Will said. "It was great. I can't remember when I've had a better time."

Judith looked at the two of them incredulously and shook her head.

"I'm thinking of doing more tours to supplement the regular business at the shop."

"Sounds like a good idea." He threw a stick for Ruby, who bounded forward for it. "You certainly are an excellent guide."

"I think if I step up the tours, I'll be able to make a decent go of it. But that won't solve my immediate problem." Clem licked her lips to keep her mouth from going dry. Asking people for money did not come easily to her. In fact, it was nearly making her sick. She had to do it, not only for her sake, but for Jess, as well.

"You mean the taxes you mentioned the other day?"

"Yes. And I was thinking, since you're a banker, and since you've said you like my jewelry work and the camping trip—well, I was wondering if you'd give me a loan."

Judith gave a derisive snort. "What kind of banker do you think—"

"This is between Clem and me," Will said, cutting Judith off.

Judith shrugged and gave them both a sour look. It looked as if she wanted to say more, and Clem couldn't help wondering what it might be.

Will looked thoughtful as he accepted the stick Ruby brought to him. Clem thought she saw a gleam come into his eye. "Hmm. Now, that's an interesting idea. You and I as partners."

Clem stopped in her tracks and had to run a step to get back in stride with them. "Partners? I wasn't looking to take on any partners. I just want a loan."

"Essentially, that's what you're doing when you take out a business loan, whether it's from a bank or an individual. When you take someone's money, they often expect a say in how you do business."

"What do you mean, exactly?" Clem asked.

"Well, as your partner, I'd ask you a lot of questions so I could analyze how you do business. Then I'd make suggestions to help you become more profitable. And I'd expect you to act on those suggestions."

"What kind of questions?" Clem tried to keep the defensiveness she was feeling from showing in her eyes. She was afraid she'd already heard it in her own voice. If Will heard it, he didn't let on.

"For example, when you explained your plan to conduct more tours, I was wondering if the tours would cut into the time you have to spend at the shop."

"Well, yes, but I kind of set my own hours, anyway. I like to come and go as I please."

"You mean the shop doesn't have regular hours?" Will gave her an incredulous look.

"What's the use in having your own business if you don't get to set your own hours? I'll bet a lot of galleries in New York are by appointment only."

"Yes, but you're not a New York gallery," offered Judith. "It sounds to me as if you should work for someone else for a while and learn some discipline before you try to run your own business." With a meaningful look at Will, she added, "If I lent you money, that's what I'd suggest."

Clem looked at the forest floor. It was so hard to make people understand her creative process. "I couldn't punch a time clock. I get my inspiration from nature, and I never know when that inspiration will strike. I have to be free to move around as I please—to go out into the woods and fields and sketch, or just be by myself. I can't live by someone else's schedule. The thought of being chained to a workbench that belongs to somebody else, turning out the same pieces of work hour after hour—it makes me crazy just thinking about it."

Apparently sensing her distress, Will said, "I'll tell you what. Why don't you write me up a business plan and I'll take a look at it. Then maybe we can work something out."

Judith rolled her eyes dramatically, but Clem ignored her. She had a chance! He'd said so. Not only did she have the opportunity to save the shop, but she was assured of seeing him again, at least once, anyway. And if he did decide to grant her the loan and become her partner as he'd said, maybe he'd want to come check on his investment from time to time, and maybe even go camping again. Clem was so happy she could have shouted. Now all she had to do was find out what a business plan was.

Will smiled, noting that Clem had begun to hold her head a little higher when he'd promised to consider her loan. If he couldn't get her to New York with him immediately, at least he could tie her to him monetarily until he could figure out a plan. He was sure that as independent as Clem was, she didn't like being indebted to anyone—he had seen the strain in her face when she'd asked him for the loan—but if she had to be indebted to someone, he'd be sure it was to him. Yes, a business partnership was a good idea. He would have to take things slow and easy with her, though, or he had a feeling she would bolt like a deer.

When they reached the cabin, Will walked Clem to her truck while Judith climbed the porch steps. Forgetting about her backpack, Judith collapsed into a rocking chair, or tried to.

"That had to hurt." Clam winced, watching Judith slide to the porch floor. "Looks as if she's going to be in physical therapy as well as psychotherapy. The phrase 'happy camper' was not coined for Judith."

"Are you kidding? I'm sure she can't wait to tell the folks at the office about coming nose-to-nose with a bear." Will's smile crinkled the corners of his eyes. He glanced back at Judith, who had righted herself, shed her pack, and slumped into the chair successfully. "She always bounces back, as they say."

Will turned to Clem again and reached out to smooth a tendril of hair away from her face. His hand slid forward and cupped her chin. "I had a great time. You're incredible. Let's talk again soon. It may take me a couple of days to work out this business deal, but after that I should be free again."

"Free," Clem murmured and nodded her head.

"See you later, wild child." Will pinched her cheek and turned toward the cabin.

Clem gazed after him, savoring the lingering sensation of his hand against her face. When he reached the door and paused to unlock it, Judith stood up, threaded her arm through his, and looked over her shoulder at Clem. The look Judith gave her wasn't just smug; it was triumphant. It irritated the hell out of Clem.

The two of them sat on Jess's front porch and laughed like fools, Clem so hard that she could hardly get the story out, and Jess until tears ran down his cheeks. Ruby napped blissfully on the top step.

"And—and then—she fell into the mudhole *again*."

"She must've thought she was snakebit, the poor

thing," wheezed the old man as he swabbed his ruddy cheeks with a bandanna.

"It was one thing right after another. I've never seen anything like it." Clem finally composed herself, only to start laughing again.

"So how'd things go other than that?"

"Really well. I talked to Will about a loan—he's some kind of banker, you know—and he said he'd think about it. So our troubles may be over. But first I have to come up with a business plan." Clem closed her eyes and breathed deeply. Uncle Jess had been baking this morning, and whatever it was smelled wonderful.

"Git from here, you rapscallion!"

Clem's eyes flew open in time to see her old pet raccoon lumbering toward the porch steps. He paused at Jess's scolding, giving Clem a solemn look.

"What'd he do this time?"

"Ate near half of a lemon pie I had cooling on the window sill. Look, he's still got meringue in his whiskers."

Sure enough, the frothy white stuff was still clinging to his snout, where his tongue couldn't reach. "Shoo. Scat. Bad Rocky." Clem waved him away. "Go bother someone else for food, why don't you?" With that, Rocky Raccoon turned curtly and waddled away.

Jess stuffed his bandanna back into the top pocket of his overalls. "So how do you like this young fella?"

Clem smiled at her uncle. Sometimes he knew her better than she knew herself. Whenever she came to him with a problem or some grand scheme, he seemed to already know about it somehow—said he could feel the "vibes." There was no such thing as keeping something from him, even if she wanted to. "I like him, Jess. He's worldly and powerful and charismatic, but he's sweet and sensitive, too. And although it sounds crazy—I mean, this man probably has everything—but I think . . ." —Clem hesitated, afraid this next part would sound silly—"he needs me."

Jess nodded in that way of his that told Clem he understood everything perfectly. Clem went on to tell her uncle about the possibility of becoming partners with Will and what it might mean—a continuing relationship, leading to where, she didn't know. Probably a dead end, since he would certainly remain in New York.

"So you like him, and he likes you. And there's a possibility, however slight, that you could have a romance with him. Now, let me ask you this." The old man propped his hand on his knee and leaned forward. "Why are you letting her have him without a fight?"

Clem returned his even gaze a long moment before her face burst into a grin. "Why, indeed?" She got up from the bench and bounded down the steps, with Ruby right behind.

"Where you going?"

"I've got to come up with a plan."

"A business plan?"

"Yeah," Clem called over her shoulder. "That, too!"

The hot bath felt like heaven. As the steam from the petal-scented water swirled around her, Clem thought about what she should do. She did some of her best thinking in the bathtub.

It came to her all at once. First, she'd call her old friend, the computer programmer and business major, and ask him what a business plan was. If there was much research involved, she'd ask him how she could do it via the Internet. Then she'd mosey down to Will's cabin and ask him very sweetly if she could use his computer—when he wasn't using it, of course. If she had to sit around the cabin waiting for him and Judith to free up some computer time, well, at least those two wouldn't be alone together. Clem pulled the chain with her toes and popped the stopper from the drain of the old clawfoot tub. *Time's a-wastin'*, she thought, reaching for a towel.

Dressed in her best jeans and shirt, Clem hopped down from the cab of the truck. It was odd that Judith's rental car wasn't there. She'd figured that they would bring it back from the wilderness store immediately, since it contained all Judith's things save what was in her backpack. Unless Clem missed her guess, Judith would have wanted to bathe and change into one of her more sophisticated outfits right away.

Hearing the sound of wood being chopped, she walked around to the back of the cabin and stopped in her tracks. Will, shirtless and in khaki shorts, brought the ax down on a piece of wood with a solid "whack," and the two ends flew apart.

The taut, rippling muscles of his shoulders and back made Clem think of Paul Bunyan. Will might not be a giant, but he was definitely the stuff of legend. He turned when he heard her approach, giving her a view of his hard, hairy chest. He glowed from a fine sheen of perspiration, and he breathed deeply and hard from his exertion. He hadn't shaved. She bit her lip to stifle a sigh, or was it a moan?

Clem saw the lazy grin spread across his face. He knew exactly what she was thinking. To hide her embarrassment, she blurted the first thing that came into her mind. "Why are you chopping wood? Isn't it too warm for a fire?"

"Maybe I just wanted a little exercise," Will said, bending to pitch the piece of wood onto the pile. He looked up at her slyly. "Or maybe I just like it hot."

Clem felt the color rise to her cheeks. He couldn't possibly look as good behind a desk as he did swinging an ax. "Where's Judith's car? I thought you'd have gone for it by now."

He put the head of the ax on the ground and leaned on its handle with both hands. "Don't you know?" His look was strange, unreadable, but the humor was still there, in his sparkling blue eyes.

"No," Clem answered tentatively. "How would I?"

Will let go of the ax handle, letting it fall to the ground. He walked slowly toward Clem. "It was a funny thing. I was in the cabin and Judith was on the porch when I heard a bloodcurdling scream. Judith came flying into the cabin shouting about how a rabid raccoon had just tried to attack her."

Clem groaned, remembering Rocky's meringue mustache. "Judith didn't happen to have any food on her, did she?"

"A peanut butter and jelly sandwich. Why?" Will's jet black brows drew together.

"Oh, nothing." On top of all Judith's other bad luck, she had just happened to be eating Rocky's favorite food.

He continued to advance on Clem. She took an involuntary step backward, then decided to hold her ground. "It seems that was the last straw," he said. "She gathered up her things and left." He stopped in front of her, his hands on his hips. There was no hint of humor in his eyes now. He looked down at her accusingly, so close she could feel his warm breath on her face.

"What?" she said defensively. "Not this again. I'm telling you, I did not sic a raccoon on Judith. Why would I do such a thing?"

"So you could have me to yourself, of course." He reached out and caught her waist between his broad hands, pulling her against him.

"Why, of all the—" Clem's indignation was quickly silenced as Will brought his lips down on hers. As he pressed her to him, she could feel all the rock-hard muscles of his chest, belly, thighs, and then some. Her knees went weak and she sagged against him. Strong arms supported her as his hands caressed her back and hips. He parted her lips, teasing and tasting her mouth with his tongue. She kissed him back, sliding her arms around his neck, responding to his every movement.

The sound of the birds, the aroma of the woods, the gentle light of the sun filtering through the trees, all faded into her subconscious. All her sensations were filled by him. The ragged rhythm of his breathing, the feel of his skin, and the clean man's scent of him blocked out all other stimuli.

Her mind was a swirl of conflicting emotions. She'd known she was falling for a man who'd be returning soon to a place where she couldn't follow. Just a few hours ago she'd expected never to see him again. Then she'd seen an opportunity to keep him in her life and she took it, impetuously, not thinking it through. And now here he was, kissing her like she'd never been kissed. Things were happening too fast.

Clem lowered her arms, letting her hands slide down to his chest, and pressed him away from her. He let her go gently, held her away from him, and looked into her eyes searchingly. She felt her body warm to him all over again.

"If you'd done that on the trip while we were alone, I probably *would* have sent a bear after *you*."

Will laughed. "Why do you think I waited? At least now I have the shelter of my cabin, and you can't leave me stranded."

Not knowing what else to do, Clem decided to bring the conversation around to the ostensible purpose of her visit. If she didn't, she was afraid he might repeat his assertion that she had wanted Judith gone just to have him all to herself. It was too close to the truth to deny. "I came to see if I could use your computer to do my business plan," she blurted. "When you're not using it, of course."

"Of course," he repeated, grinning.

As Clem led the way to the cabin, Will watched the gentle sway of her hips. He was delighted by her request to use the computer because of the opportunity to be alone with her again, but he couldn't get carried away. The kiss had been fantastic. He wasn't put off by her skittishness—in fact, he'd expected it. He had a feeling that if he came on too strong she might bolt for the woods, so he'd bide his time. He hadn't gotten to be the king of Wall Street by having bad timing. He was famous for his uncanny ability to know just when to make his move, and he knew the time wasn't right, yet.

Once inside the cabin, Will had Clem sit at the computer while he dragged up a chair and sat close behind her. "Have you ever used a computer?" he asked, pressing the ON switch on the side of the processing unit.

"No. The little mountain school I went to didn't have them." Will leaned closer and, reaching around

her, took her right hand in his and placed it on top
of the mouse. With his hand still over hers, he put
the mouse through its paces until a bright blue
screen appeared. Clem was leaning against his chest
now. Learning had never been this much fun.

The computer beeped. "What's that noise?" Clem
asked.

"I've got mail. See that little icon at the bottom of
the screen?" Will clicked the mouse, and an electronic message filled the screen. He scanned it
quickly and bit his lip to keep himself from shouting
an obscenity right in Clem's ear. Judith hadn't been
creating a diversion with her story about the Carter
account. It was for real, and this memo contained
even more urgent information than Judith had
known. He could not handle the situation by phone
and fax, as he'd hoped. There was no help for it; he
had to go back to New York. *Damn.*

"It's not good, is it?"

"No, sweetheart, it's not." Will took his hand from
the mouse and caressed her shoulder, hugging her
to his chest. "I have to go back to the city, but it'll
only be for a few days." She said nothing, didn't beg
him to stay as he would have liked but would never
have expected. Her reflection in the monitor be-
trayed her, though, and told him everything he
wanted, needed, to know. She was visibly upset.

"I should go," she murmured.

"No, stay while I get my things together. I'll get
you into an Internet site that can give you information on business plans. Then go back to the word
processing program and start a new file for your
document. That'll keep you busy until I'm ready to
go." It would also give him time to think.

He retreated to the other side of the cabin, where

he slid the suitcase out from under the bed and began throwing things into it. Part of him wanted to ask her, beg her if necessary, to go with him. A week ago, the thought of begging a woman to do anything would have appalled him. Now it seemed perfectly reasonable, except for the fact that it wouldn't work.

He watched her as she pecked tentatively at the keyboard. She looked so vulnerable, her hair now in a ponytail hanging down her slender back. He remembered the nightmare she'd had, and her fear of the city. He couldn't ask her to go to New York with him now. It wasn't the right time. Maybe if she had a compelling reason to go there later, and time to get used to the idea . . . A thought struck him, and he smiled at the simplicity of it.

When Will was satisfied he had packed all he needed, he went back to Clem's side. "Clem, I have an idea. Why don't I take a selection of your jewelry to New York and take it to a gallery or two? I'm sure I could generate some interest in a show. It could be the answer to all your financial problems."

Clem looked at him incredulously. "You're kidding. My work in a New York art gallery? My work isn't sophisticated enough—not . . . *artsy* enough. They'd laugh you right out of the place."

"No. You're wrong. Your work is wonderful."

Clem looked at him as if she thought he might be teasing her. "Absolutely not. I prefer to sell it myself, anyway. That's half the fun—meeting people and talking to them."

Will sighed, deciding to drop the gallery idea. For now. "Here's a spare key to the cabin. I want you to feel free to use the computer all you like. And here's my business card with my phone number. I'll be back in a few days, and we'll take up where we left off. On the business plan, and whatever else comes up." He gave her his most reassuring smile as he held out the key and card to her.

Her expression told him clearly that she didn't believe him. She looked up at him, bright-eyed and blinking back the threatening tears, and it nearly broke his heart.

"Why would you bother to come back here?" she asked quietly.

Will put the key and the card on the computer table, sat opposite her, and took both her hands in his. "I came to these mountains to figure things out," he began, looking deeply into her jade eyes. "And in the time I've been here, I've only managed to come up with more questions. I have to come back, to get some answers to those questions."

Her mouth quivered almost imperceptibly. "What questions?"

"Well, for starters . . ." Will said, reaching out and cupping her chin, "how do you tame a wild child?"

Will gripped the steering wheel of his rental car savagely. Leaving Clem alone there in his cabin was the hardest thing he'd ever done. He might have felt a little better if he had only been able to come up with a plan for eventually getting her to New York, but he had gotten nowhere with the gallery idea. If she'd only agreed, he could have set up a show for her and insisted she come to Manhattan for the occasion. As her business partner, he could demand that she try to reach a wider audience.

She had said no. How did he get around that? As long as it was her jewelry and he had not yet given her the loan making them partners, it was her decision. What if it were *his* jewelry? How could she possibly object if he bought the jewelry himself? Her refusal to let him take the pieces to a gallery was just based on a fear of rejection, anyway, and he knew her work would not be rejected. He knew just the gallery he would go to. Elaine would adore Clem's work.

Within a few minutes he was pulling into the driveway of Clem's shop. He desperately hoped that Clem's Uncle Jess would be minding the store in her absence. The only vehicle at the shop was a three-wheeled motorcycle of some sort. Will took the steps in two bounds.

The old man was sweeping the floor, leaning on the broom for support as much as he was sweeping with it. Before Will could introduce himself, Jess said, "You must be Will Fletcher."

"Yes. How'd you know?"

Jess waved his hand as if the question was of no consequence. He'd seen Clem use the same dismissive gesture a dozen times, not to mention the intuition. This was her uncle, all right.

"Cup of coffee?"

"No, thanks." Will paused, considering the best approach to his task. He could let the old man in on his plan, or he could just buy the jewelry and say nothing. His hunch, and it was only that, was that he should come clean to Uncle Jess.

"I guess Clem mentioned that she and I were considering becoming partners." Will crossed his fingers. A positive response would make this transaction go a whole lot easier.

"She said something about it," Jess said warily, leaning the broom against the wall.

Will let out a long breath. "I've just about decided

to grant her the loan she wants. But first I'd like to take some of her jewelry to New York. A friend of mine owns a gallery, and I think she'll love Clem's work. I'll pay you for it now, of course. I have that much confidence in Clem's talent." Will gave Jess his best salesman's smile.

Jess slowly closed his arthritic fingers around a coffee cup sitting on the counter. "Does Clem know about this?"

"Well, she wasn't actually in favor of the idea. But I figured if I bought the jewelry myself, to demonstrate my good faith, she'd go along with the idea. You see, I have to return to New York on urgent business, but I'll be back in a few days. The idea of going ahead with the plan just came to me in the car. I thought maybe you could tell her for me."

The old man snorted, almost choking on a swallow of coffee. "That's easy for you to say. When I tell her, you'll be safe at thirty thousand feet, and I'll be down here getting my ass chewed off."

Will had to laugh. "I understand, believe me. But as Clem's new partner, I think her work should be seen by a wider audience. I'm afraid I'm going to have to insist on that."

"Oh, you insist, do you?"

Will held his breath. He hoped he hadn't gone too far with the authoritative approach. Just as he was trying to think of a way to mollify Jess, the old man broke out into a wide grin. "I'll just tell her that, too. And when she blows her stack, even thirty thousand feet isn't going to be high enough to save your hide."

Will thought he saw the wheels turning in Jess's mind. He was undoubtedly weighing the consequences of whatever action he chose to take. He stood with one hand in the pocket of his overalls and scratched his head. Finally, something seemed to dawn on him and he grinned again.

"All right. You can have whatever you want, and I'll accept your payment for it. If she doesn't like what you've done, that'll be between you and her."

Relieved, Will nodded his agreement. He decided to let the old man in on the rest of his plan to give Clem a chance to get used to the idea while he was gone. "I just know that this gallery owner will like Clem's work so much that she'll want to feature it in a show. That'll be a big event, so of course Clem will have to come to Manhattan for it."

"Of course." Jess smiled pleasantly, already unlocking the display case.

Will watched as Jess began taking Clem's jewelry out of the case. Funny, he'd expected more of a reaction out of the old man when he mentioned Clem coming to New York. It was as if Jess were a step ahead of him. Instinctively, and against his better judgment, he decided to press his luck with Jess further. "You know, I'm really fond of Clem."

The old man looked up from his task and fixed on Will a look of paternal concern and a touch of warning. He was putting Clem's creations, each separated by layers of tissue paper, in a box.

"And I respect her," Will continued hastily. "As her uncle, what would you advise? That is, what would you say to a man who wanted to get close to Clem?"

Jess closed the lid on the box with a snap. "Good luck."

Clem's thoughts were in turmoil. Will was definitely interested in her. The thought was both thrilling and terrifying. What would happen when he came back? Would she continue her free fall into love or lust or whatever it was she was feeling for a man she couldn't have?

And what was *he* thinking? She'd made it clear to him that she couldn't, wouldn't, live in an urban environment. Did he consider her a summer romance? Even worse, did he consider a sexual relationship part of their potential business arrangement? No, she knew him well enough now to know he wasn't that kind of man. The big question was, what had he meant by his last statement before he left the cabin?

The memory of his kiss came back to her like flowing honey, sweet and slow. She closed her eyes and relived the feeling of his mouth on hers, his hands molding their bodies together. A few days, he'd said, and then he'd be back. *More kisses.*

Sighing, she opened her eyes again and looked out the window at the summer afternoon. She longed to be out there now. Sitting at this desk reminded her of school, which she'd hated, but she had to finish this plan. She wanted to do a good job so that he would know that she was smart and capable. His opinion mattered more and more to her all the time.

After she typed her business description and goals, she reached in her pocket for the notes she had taken when she called her friend the computer genius earlier. She switched computer programs and typed the phone number of an online business information service. Her friend had told her it would be a good source.

She browsed through the topics on the bulletin board, making occasional notes. She was just about to skip over a group of messages about the rumored acquisition of one company by another when she saw something that caught her eye. Wasn't Carter Industries the client company that Will and Judith had been talking about? In case this was something he might be interested in, she clicked the PRINT button.

Clem returned to the shop right before closing time. She was tired, but satisfied with what she'd accomplished so far. She had a solid beginning on the business plan. Jess lounged at the workbench, thumbing through a seed catalog.

Clem waved the computer printout of her half-finished plan in the air. "Will had to leave, but I got a good start on the . . ." Her voice trailed off as she noticed the empty spaces in the display case. "Where's all my stuff?" As Clem continued around the L-shaped display to get to the workbench in the center, she saw even more of her work missing. Then she saw the charge slip by the cash register. As she snatched it up, her eye fell on the fine, fluid signature of William B. Fletcher. "What the hell is going on here?"

Jess put the catalog down and took a deep breath. "He bought it all. Said he was going to take it to an art gallery in New York. When I asked him if you were in on the plan, he said that since you were going to be partners and all, he felt like he had a right to make this move on his own."

Apparently determined not to let her get a word in edgewise until he had spilled the whole story, Jess took another quick breath and continued. "He said that even though you disagreed with him about taking the pieces to New York, he insisted on it, anyway."

Jess fanned himself with the catalog, as if the effort of telling the story had wrung him out, and visibly steeled himself for her reaction.

"Ooh! Of all the nerve!" Clem's face reddened to the tips of her ears, and she balled her hands into fists at her sides. "I distinctly told him that I did not want him to take my work to galleries. So he went against my wishes and decided to completely change how I market my work. I can't believe this guy!" Clem felt desolate as the warmth she had felt toward Will ebbed away.

"What if he can't sell it? He'll probably want his money back. What am I supposed to do then? The summer festival is coming up next week. It's the most traffic we'll get all year, and if I don't have the jewelry I can't take advantage of it. I'll be in worse trouble than I'm in now."

Jess pointed to the charge slip. "Don't give him a refund."

"You don't think for a second that I'll actually accept that money, do you?"

"Why not?"

"Because I'm not a charity case, and I'm perfectly capable of marketing my own work in my own way." Clem began pacing up and down in front of the workbench where Jess sat with his hands folded over the bib of his overalls.

"He said he had faith in your work," Jess said, rubbing his chin. "He didn't seem to think that he'd have any trouble getting you a gallery show."

"A gallery show! Those New York art snobs aren't going to give me a show. Unless . . ." Clem stopped pacing, a horrified look crossing her face.

"What?"

"I know what he'll do," she said with an awful certainty. "He'll market me as a folk artist. A primitive folk artist. Northerners love to buy handicrafts that they imagine were made by little old ladies in some southern backwater."

"You're being paranoid and ridiculous," Jess said firmly. "You're a silversmith and a lapidary, and a fine one, at that. Why do you have to put yourself down?"

"You don't understand."

"I know you're afraid of being made fun of like you were when you were a kid, but—"

"I'm not afraid of anything," Clem said sharply.

The old man smiled slyly. "Oh, yeah? I'll bet you're afraid to go to New York and get your jewelry back."

Clem gaped, her eyes round, her heart pounding. She started to protest, but she couldn't. He'd gotten her, the old coot. A sudden chill came over her, and she rubbed her arms. Could she really go to New York alone? How hard could it be? It wasn't as if she'd be trapped in the city, unable to escape, like she'd been before. She needed that jewelry. If he weren't back in a few days as he'd promised, or if he came back without the stuff, she was in trouble. Taking *his* money was out of the question now that he'd proven himself to be a sneaky, underhanded, lowdown snake. She wanted nothing more to do with him.

Jess put his hands on his knees and leaned forward. "I dare you."

That did it.

Jess strolled out on the porch and chuckled as he watched Clem tear out of the driveway, her truck tires raising a spray of gravel as they went. She'd never been able to resist a dare. He was glad he hadn't mentioned Will's threat to require her to go to New York. That girl was so contrary that if she thought he'd try to force her to go, you couldn't get her there with wild horses.

He hoped he hadn't made a mistake encouraging her, however slyly, to take the trip. New York could be a dangerous place, after all.

EIGHT

Will walked into the Soho art gallery and paused to look around and above him. He never ceased to be amazed at what Elaine came up with. This time it was yards and yards of colorful fabrics, arranged in no discernible pattern, billowing across the ceiling. He craned his neck to study the work, and after a minute or so he became aware of someone standing at his elbow.

"So, what do you think?" asked a petite woman in a cultured, New England accent.

"That depends. What's it supposed to be?"

"It doesn't have to *be* something." Her tone of exasperation was tempered by fondness. She always knew when he was baiting her. "Haven't I taught you anything?"

"You've taught me not to make fun of your artists, for fear of getting my ears boxed."

"I've never once boxed your ears, but I might've if I could have reached them."

Will smiled down at his old friend. Elaine Stuart, owner of the Stuart Gallery, was an elegant older woman, her small, wiry figure reminiscent of the dancer she had once been. Her black hair, with its wings of gray at the temples, was pulled back into a bun, as usual. The severity of her simple black dress was tempered only by the dramatic silver and turquoise jewelry at her ears, throat, and wrists. When he was a boy, Will thought Elaine was the very soul of class and sophistication. He was in awe of her, both then and now.

Elaine linked her arm through his as they strolled to her office. "Let's have some tea and chat. It's been weeks since you've come to see me. What's in the case?"

"Something you're going to love."

Will followed Elaine into her neat, small office. In front of the desk was a small area with a chair, loveseat, and coffee table. As Elaine poured the tea, Will explained how he'd met Clem. He opened the case and spread the pieces out on the coffee table, watching for Elaine's reaction. Her eyebrows arched in surprise at first, and then a slow smile spread across her face as she picked up each piece, examining the workmanship.

"Lovely designs. So different, so fresh. And so well-made. She really knows how to showcase a stone to its full potential. When do I get to meet her so we can put a show together?"

Will relaxed. She was sold, just as he'd known she would be. "That could be a bit of a problem. You see, she has a hangup about the city. She doesn't want to come here."

Elaine put on one of the bracelets, admiring it against her olive skin. "Poor dear. So she's a country girl who's never been to a big city?"

"Not exactly. Long story."

Elaine's gaze went from the jewelry to Will's face, an inquisitive look in her eyes and a half-smile playing about her lips. "You're the last person in the world I would have expected to see come in here and pitch an artist's work. You obviously are taking quite a personal interest in this young woman."

"We've become friends." Will took a long sip of tea. Since his parents died, nobody had known him very well—except Elaine. A close friend of his parents, Elaine was like a mother to him now, the only person he ever confided in. There wasn't much point in keeping things from her—she'd figure them out, anyway. The look in her hawkish black eyes told him he'd better come clean. "She's very special. Unlike anyone I've ever known. I'd like to try to get her to come to New York to live with me for a while. To see if what I'm feeling is . . . the real thing."

"And what is *she* feeling?" Elaine looked at him over the rim of the bone china cup.

"I guess we'll find that out, too," he said. "All I know right now is that I want her with me."

She smiled at him inquisitively. "She must be special indeed if she overcame your aversion for artists. The only reason you ever come to my showings is to make business contacts."

"I do not dislike all artists." Will set his cup down on its saucer. "I've always been crazy about you. I used to beg my parents to take me with them to see you dance."

Elaine drew herself up proudly. "That was when you were a boy. Ever since your parents lost the family fortune on that artists' community venture, you've distrusted anyone with a creative side."

A bitter taste came to Will's mouth as he remembered the incident. His parents had squandered the last of the money they'd inherited on the ill-conceived scheme. Over the years they'd let themselves be talked into many such ventures. It seemed they could never say no when an artist needed money for a project. Art had been their passion—and their downfall.

"They should have put you at the helm," he said brightly, trying to shake off his sudden, negative mood. "Then even that boondoggle would have made money."

"That's true, but beside the point. And flattery will get you nowhere." Elaine smiled and wagged her index finger at him in mock warning. "The point is, I'm delighted that you've finally found someone who makes you happy. I was beginning to wonder if you ever would. And I'm thrilled that she's an artist. What poetic justice."

Will rolled his eyes. "Oh, no. I've only just learned to appreciate art. Don't go bringing poetry into it."

Elaine clasped her hands together and laughed so heartily the bangles at her wrists made a pleasant, jingling music.

Clem stepped off the bus onto Manhattan pavement and into a whole new world. As she waded through the sea of fellow travellers in the Port Authority bus terminal and out onto the street, she felt shoved toward a wall of sound. She was assaulted by excited voices talking in foreign languages, honking horns, jackhammers, steel doors slamming, street peddlers hawking their wares. Dozens more sounds blended together, impossible to identify or even isolate.

She looked at the people around her, people of all descriptions. How could they stand the noise? Some rushed by, as if they were late for important events in their lives, and others loitered, oblivious to time and, apparently, their surroundings.

The long ride combined with the sensory overload had made her dizzy, and she leaned against a trash can for support, clutching her small duffle bag. How did anyone ever take in all this? As she took a deep, calming breath, the smells of automobile exhaust mingled with a dozen other odors she couldn't identify. There was food cooking somewhere, too, she thought, rubbing her empty stomach. She'd find something to eat as soon as she could, but first she had to find Will Fletcher.

As she gathered her courage she continued to lean on the trash can as if it were the only thing tethered to a world spinning out of control. She watched an elderly woman step from the curb to the street and hold up her arm. Within a few moments, a Yellow Cab stopped and the woman got in. Hailing a cab looked easy enough. Clem took another deep breath and started to the curb.

When she reached the street, she held out her arm, and a cab stopped for her. Clem got in, put her bag at her feet, and showed the gray-haired driver the address on Will's business card.

Clem settled back and tried to relax. She had no idea where she was going or how long the trip would take. The cab was old but clean, although the tree-shaped air freshener dangling from the rearview mirror couldn't quite clear out the odor of cigar smoke left by a recent passenger.

The cab made two right turns and headed south. Clem saw men wheeling racks and racks of clothing along the sidewalks, some toward waiting trucks. Shop windows displayed beads, buttons, lace, and trimmings.

The cab slowed to a near stop behind a traffic backup, and the driver craned his neck to see what the holdup was. After a few seconds, he shrugged and veered the cab sharply to the left, down a side street that was little more than an alley. At the next block they stopped at a traffic light, and Clem looked at the building on her right. Surrounded by a ten-foot wall, it appeared to be a residential building of some sort. The top of the wall was lined with broken bottles of all shapes and sizes, their jagged shards jutting toward the sky. Clem shivered. She couldn't imagine living in a prison like that.

As they continued downtown, Clem marveled at the bustling street life of the different neighborhoods. She liked the colorful eccentricity of Greenwich Village and the boutiques of Soho. The cab veered east, and she saw a glimpse of Little Italy's sidewalk cafés and Chinatown's colorful storefronts and restaurants.

As they continued south, the buildings changed to skyscrapers, and the streets took a more random pattern, cutting across each other at odd angles. As the buildings grew larger and more imposing, Clem grew more apprehensive. By the time the driver pulled up to the curb in front of a particularly menacing concrete and steel monolith, she was more anxious than ever.

Clem counted out the driver's fare and tip and got out of the cab. Looking up at the forbidding structure that seemed to touch the clouds, she was seized by the urge to run, to ask the driver to take her back to the bus station. She squared her shoulders and tried to summon the indignation she'd felt when she found out that Will Fletcher had taken her jewelry. It worked. Her feet began to carry her toward the entrance.

She approached the revolving door, its glass and

steel panels coming at her one after another like the teeth of some mythic monster. Finally, she swallowed her fear and jumped into one of the compartments. A second later she came out with a *whoosh* into a lobby with a polished marble floor and several banks of elevators. The building directory told her that Will's suite was on the fortieth floor, so she went to the elevator and waited.

Men and women in conservative business attire and briefcases walked briskly by her, acknowledging neither her nor each other. Feeling that she might as well be invisible, she checked her reflection in the elevator doors. She was still there, all right, although severely underdressed in her best jeans and simple cotton shirt.

The elevator seemed to take forever before depositing Clem at her destination. She could have sworn she felt her ears pop from the altitude. Taking a deep breath, she looked around her. The foyer led to double glass doors which bore the name and logo of Will's company in elegant gold letters. The large reception area had lush, teal-colored carpeting and drapes with chairs and sofas of a matching print.

Clem paused long enough to unzip her bag and remove a sheaf of papers. Even though she wouldn't be taking any of Will's money, she wanted to prove to him that she could write a business plan, so she'd taken time to complete it before she had left for New York. She also had the printout of the information she'd run across on Will's business deal.

A rosewood reception desk stood guard in front of a partition, beyond which lay the inner offices. A stern but stylish looking woman sat behind the desk, a telephone pressed to one ear. Clem stood before her, intending to ask to see Will as soon as the woman

finished her phone call. The receptionist peered over
the glasses that perched on the end of her nose and
beckoned to Clem. Puzzled, Clem came closer.

"Well, what are you waiting for? Give me the package."

Clem looked around her. "What package?"

The woman gestured toward Clem's bag. "You *are*
a courier, aren't you?"

"No. I'm here to see Will Fletcher."

The woman looked Clem up and down and sniffed.
"Do you have an appointment?"

"Not exactly, but I—"

Clem froze as a familiar figure appeared from behind the partition. Judith, even more impeccably
turned out than she had been when Clem first saw
her, wore an elegant navy suit and white silk blouse.
When she saw Clem, she stopped abruptly beside the
desk. Her face clearly displayed a rapid succession of
emotions, registering shock only briefly. Confusion
followed, replaced by anger, and finally a benign, if
wary, tolerance.

"Clem, I'm surprised to see you here."

"I'm pretty surprised to be here."

"Will didn't tell me you were coming." Judith
tilted her head inquisitively. Clem had a feeling she
would not get past the desk until she'd explained
herself to Judith.

"He doesn't know I'm here. I just got into town.
Listen, I need to talk to him. It won't take long. I
have to give him this business plan, and get some
things of mine that he has. Then I'll be on my way."

Judith's smile was full of condescending sweetness.
"You poor dear. Don't tell me he actually made you
go through with writing a business plan."

"He said the plan was to let the investors know that

I was a good risk, that my business was worth investing in," said Clem warily.

"Clem, Will's clients do not invest in small mom-and-pop businesses. They invest in huge companies, sometimes whole countries. If Will loans you money, it will be from out of his own pocket."

"But he said he was a banker," Clem said, shocked and confused.

"He's an *investment* banker. He handles issues of stock for large corporations. His average transactions are in the millions." Judith reached out and gently patted Clem's shoulder as one would comfort an unhappy child.

Clem jerked away. How could she have made such a stupid, ignorant mistake? She'd never been more mortified in her life and, looking into the other woman's eyes, she was certain that Judith knew it. Judith's smug expression spoke volumes. Clem had been a party to Judith's most humiliating moments when they were on Clem's turf. Now they were in Judith's domain, as strange to Clem as the wilderness had been to Judith. Turnabout was fair play, and Judith relished it.

"Ginger, I can vouch for this woman. She's a friend of Mr. Fletcher's." Although Judith spoke to the receptionist, she never took her eyes off Clem. "I'm sure he'll want to know she's here."

Ginger looked down at the maze of blinking lights on her telephone's control panel. "He's on the phone now," she said hesitantly.

Judith smiled in that cloying way of hers. "I have a great idea. I was just in his office. The call's not that important, believe me. I want you to show Miss Harper in to see him unannounced. What a great surprise that would be."

Ginger looked skeptical. "Are you sure? I—"

"I insist," Judith said with finality.

Clem had no doubt of what Judith was playing at. Judith knew Clem was struggling for control, blinking back tears. The woman wanted her to have to face Will this way, before she'd regained her composure. Clem had no idea what she'd do when she was face-to-face with Will, but she was determined that Judith would not have the satisfaction of seeing her cry.

"Thank you, Judith. I'm sure Will and I can clear up this misunderstanding in no time. Then I'll run along."

"I'm sure you can. I guess this is good-bye, then." Smiling pleasantly now, Judith extended her hand and Clem shook it briefly. "Take care of yourself." With that, Judith left the outer office and disappeared down a hallway.

The receptionist hung up the phone and came around the desk, beckoning Clem to follow her. Clem did what she was told, hoping the receptionist didn't notice that her breath now came in hitching gasps. They walked down a plush carpeted hallway, the walls of which were hung with the portraits of sour-looking old men—the firms' forefathers, Clem guessed. She shrank from their stern, silent stares as she passed by one after the other.

After what seemed like forever, the receptionist stopped before a pair of mahogany double doors. Pushing through one of them, she motioned Clem into the office, then retreated.

Will stood with his back to her, looking out at a breathtaking view of lower Manhattan. One hand held a phone to his ear and the other rested on his hip. His jacket was off and his sleeves were rolled up. He stood with feet braced apart and shoulders squared, poised for battle, it seemed. He radiated confidence and authority. At that moment, feeling as she did, Clem hated him for it. She hated herself even more, because her body tingled with longing at the sight of him.

"I'll have someone get back to you on this, Roberts." Will hung up the phone and stretched like a huge predator after a good meal. Clem had once thought he could never look as good behind a desk as he did in the mountains, but she'd been wrong. He was king of this jungle, and he oozed raw power.

She knew she should announce herself, but she was paralyzed, unable to speak. Then he turned around, as if in slow motion, each frame frozen in time. His face turned to pure joy as he saw her. Charging out from behind his desk, he came to her and wrapped his arms tightly around her.

"Clem, I'm so glad you came. I hoped you would."

Clem did not return his embrace, but stood rigidly. He'd hoped she'd come? On top of everything else, had he deliberately lured her to New York?

"Where's my jewelry?"

"What?" Will held her away from him and looked into her face.

"You heard me. I want my jewelry back. You had no right to take it after I told you not to." She shrugged out of his grasp and backed a step away from him. "Just because you bought the stuff yourself doesn't give you the right to go against my wishes."

Will let her go, apparently well aware now that she was furious. "I explained to your uncle why I needed to take the jewelry. If you're going to sell more of your work, you have to have it seen by more people."

"That's beside the point," Clem said, still clutching the strap of her bag in one hand and the papers in the other. "I can't believe you took it on yourself to completely change the way I do business. I explained to you why I like things the way they are."

"Clem, the way things are isn't working. You've admitted as much. You know as well as I do that the real reason you didn't want your work taken to a gallery was because you thought they'd make fun of you." Will reached for her again, but she took another step back. He seemed to be searching for the right words to placate her. "But that didn't happen. In fact, I got you a show. Isn't that great?"

A show. Clem's head was beginning to throb. The promise of a show was probably a smokescreen, just like the business plan—a way for him to manipulate her. "Why should I believe you? How do I know this isn't just a come-on?"

"Why would I lie about something like that?" Will looked genuinely hurt, and more than a little angry.

"To get me to come to New York."

His eyes searched her face and he took a deep breath, as if to calm himself. "I won't deny that I've thought about having you come to New York, at least for a while. But I would never lie to you."

"Oh, no? What about the business plan?"

"What about it?"

"You said it was for investors to see if I could run a successful business, but you had no intention of showing it to any investors, did you?" Clem studied his face while this charge sank in. There was a chance Judith had been lying, but she didn't think so.

Will's anger seemed to dissipate, but not his frustration. A muscle in his jaw tightened. "Clem, I'd be the only investor. If I led you to believe there would be others, I'm sorry. I did say we'd be partners if I made you the loan."

Clem grudgingly admitted to herself that this last part was true. Had she only misunderstood him? The throbbing in her head was like a jackhammer, and gnawing hunger made her stomach feel almost as bad as her head. The fact that she'd made such a fool of herself made her feel even more wretched than that. And to make matters worse, she didn't know how to feel about Will anymore.

Was he trying to make her beholden to him with the personal loan? Did he take her jewelry against her wishes to lure her to New York? Was the show just a come-on? She was only certain of one thing. To take money from a man who would expect heaven-knew-what in return was out of the question—especially when it was a man who had no more regard for her feelings or her judgment than to try to revamp her business without discussing it with her first.

She knew one more thing. She had to get out of there. Now. Just as Will reached out for her again, she said, "I'm not taking money from someone I don't trust. I don't want a loan from you, and I don't want to be partners with you. Now, tell me where my jewelry is."

Will looked stricken, a shadow falling across his handsome features. "Can't we talk about this? We could meet for dinner and—"

"No. Now where's my stuff?"

Will went to his desk and Clem followed him, thinking the jewelry was in a drawer. Instead, he removed a business card from a drawer and handed it to her. "This is the gallery where I took your jewelry. The owner is a friend of mine. She's the one who wants to give you the show." He grasped her shoulder, squeezing it gently. "Clem, promise me that you'll listen to what Elaine has to say to you."

Clem looked at the card, then back up at Will. Part of her still wanted to believe that his intentions were good. "We'll see. By the way, even though I'm not taking your money, I finished the business plan, anyway—just so you'd know I had the gumption to do it." Clem dropped the papers on the desk and turned to leave, slinging her bag over her shoulder.

"Wait," he called after her. "At least tell me where you're staying."

"Can't," she said, not turning back. She couldn't tell because she didn't know.

As soon as she got beyond the double doors, she turned down the hallway and sprinted past the mean old men and their surly stares. The snooty receptionist Ginger was rounding the corner from her desk just as Clem reached the point where the hallway came out into the outer office. As Clem ran squarely into her, the stack of memos in Ginger's hands made like so much confetti, fluttering upward and outward. "Oof," Ginger gasped, spinning around on the heel of one smartly polished pump.

Clem didn't slow down until she reached the elevator, and not much even then. Although the doors were closing, she managed to throw herself and her bag through the opening, eliciting stares from the six people already aboard.

Clem eased herself into the corner nearest her and looked from one to the other. "Urgent delivery," she said solemnly, patting her bag. The strangers turned their attention to the row of electronic lights near the ceiling, and she was invisible again.

Back out on the street, she felt palpable relief to be away from Will and his office. She didn't even mind the raindrops that began to strike her face with increasing frequency. Clem looked around for an overhang of some sort, but the only shelter was in front of the dreaded revolving door. She was afraid if she got too close to its gaping maw, she'd be sucked into that awful building again.

With a sigh of resignation, she glanced at the address on the gallery business card and began the difficult task of hailing a cab in the rain.

Clem shouldered her bag and stepped inside the Stuart Gallery. She was glad to see it was less intimidating than the last building she'd been in. In fact, it was delightful. The walls were adorned with paintings, some provocative in their boldness, others with more subtle charm. In one corner was a display of blown glass in shapes and colors so fantastic Clem longed to touch them but dared not. Every nook and cranny held an exhibit more enchanting than the last.

The best had to be the ceiling. Above her head, wispy clouds of color billowed in a gently whispering breeze. Clem couldn't believe how much she liked this, this *thing*. It was like nothing she'd ever seen. After a few moments of looking straight up, she decided on a more practical approach. Selecting an out-of-the-way spot behind a large piece of sculpture, Clem lay down on the floor and admired the artwork. She studied its textures, its color gradations, its lines.

"What a wonderful idea," someone said from behind her. Clem's first instinct was to vault upward to her feet, but she didn't, and couldn't have said why. Instead she twisted her head slightly to see who'd spoken and looked up into the angular, smiling face of an elegant-looking older woman.

"I think I'm going to encourage everyone to view it that way. If my arthritis didn't make getting up and down so difficult, I'd try it myself."

Clem didn't know if the woman was sincere or only trying to make her feel less awkward, but she was grateful either way. Clem slowly rose to her feet. "I really like it," she said sheepishly.

"I'm glad. I like it, too." The woman extended her hand. "I'm Elaine Stuart.

Clem shook her hand gingerly, mindful of the painful condition that had left the older woman's fingers bent like her uncle's. "I'm Clem Harper."

"I've been expecting you." Elaine led the way to her office, decorated much more conservatively than Clem would have imagined, judging by the exhibits in the gallery. Elaine indicated that Clem was to sit on the loveseat. On the coffee table was a large chunk of amethyst crystal.

Elaine followed Clem's gaze to the crystal. "I'm partial to pretty rocks, too, as you can see. Would you like some tea?"

"Yes, please," Clem said gratefully. Thirsty, wet, and hungry as she was, hot tea sounded like nectar of the gods. She leaned forward to touch the craggy, purple surfaces of the amethyst, running her fingers through the peaks and valleys there. "This is a nice specimen."

Thanks. I've had it for ages. Cream and sugar?" Elaine poured tea into two china cups from a silver service on a side table.

"Lots of both, thanks." Clem's empty stomach made a sound and she clapped her hand over it, grateful that Elaine's back was turned. As the older woman reached for the ornate cream pitcher, Clem wondered how to ask for her jewelry without being rude. She couldn't very well say, "Some jewelry of mine was given to you under false pretenses, and I want it back." Or maybe she should. Elaine set a cup of tea in front of her and took the chair opposite her. Clem took a sip of the tea, savoring its warmth and sweet, full flavor.

"Your work is exquisite," Elaine said simply. "Where did you study?"

"Thanks," Clem murmured, completely surprised by the woman's forthright praise. "I'm mostly self-taught.

"Well, then, I'm doubly impressed."

Clem was feeling better already. Whether it was from the tea or from Elaine's remarks, she didn't know. She watched the other woman study her over the rim of her teacup. Her midnight black hair was pulled back severely. That, plus her simple, black clothing, reminded Clem of the beatniks she had seen in old fifties movies. She looked just the way Clem thought a gallery owner should look. More than that, her compact size belied a charisma, a strength of character, that was almost tangible.

"Your designs are delightful—so original. And your silversmithing skills are excellent. But most of all, I really admire the way you use the stones."

Clem could hardly believe her ears. This was most likely the woman who'd selected that wonderful collection of artwork she'd just seen. She wondered for a moment if Elaine's glowing assessment of her was a put-up job, orchestrated by Will. The more she looked at Elaine Stuart, the more she realized that the woman was sincere. Clem doubted if even Will Fletcher could talk this woman into such a scheme.

"Thanks," Clem said softly.

Elaine put her teacup on its saucer and leaned back, folding her arthritic hands in front of her. "What's your inspiration? For your designs, I mean?"

The question was a refreshing change from the money-oriented ones that Will and the other bankers had asked her. It was great to talk to someone who was interested in her creative process.

"Nature," she said. "I guess it's my Native American background. I just feel close to nature."

Elaine nodded her understanding. "I want to include your work in a show. Are you interested?"

Clem let out a deep breath. Will hadn't been lying, after all. It was real. Looking into the intense gaze of Elaine Stuart, she knew this wasn't a game, and she felt a pang of guilt for the things she'd thought about Will. "I don't know if you know this, but Will took my work from my shop without my permission. I hadn't planned to try to get a gallery show. I'll have to think about it."

"That's understandable. But I'll need to know in the next couple of days. My next show is in two weeks, and you'd be part of that. Where are you staying?"

"I don't know yet," Clem said, and a new wave of anxiety hit her. Not only did she not know what she would do about the show, but she didn't even know where she was going to spend the night. "Can I call you? I have your card."

"Fine," Elaine said, smiling. "I'll be looking forward to hearing from you. Your work will be safe here while you decide."

Figuring their interview was over, Clem put down her teacup and stood up. "Could you tell me where I could get something to eat?"

"Two blocks up, there's a sidewalk café that's pretty

good," Elaine said, rising from her chair with an effort. Clem thanked her and turned to go.

"You must be very special to Will."

The older woman's statement stopped Clem in her tracks. She turned silently and looked once again into Elaine's frank gaze.

"He's a good boy," Elaine said. "Way too focused on practical things, mind you. Things like stocks, bonds, futures, that sort of thing. He needs a little magic in his life."

Clem smiled and said good-bye. She stepped outside the gallery and into bright sunshine. The rain had given the street a freshly washed look, making everything seem brand new.

If she wanted it, she would have a real New York art gallery show, but that wasn't what was making her heart beat overtime. It was the other thing that Elaine had said. Clem Harper was very special to Will Fletcher.

NINE

Clem sat at one of the sidewalk café's small, wrought iron tables savoring her first ever cup of cappuccino and trying to sort out her feelings. The sunshine and good food had improved her mood considerably, not to mention the wonderful things Elaine had said about her work. Best of all, Elaine had confirmed that the show was legitimate. Will hadn't lied to her about that, after all.

Perhaps he hadn't really lied about the loan, either. She supposed it was possible that she'd misunderstood him about the investors. As far as taking her jewelry to a gallery was concerned, maybe that had been for the best, after all. She'd seen the prices on some of those pieces at the gallery. If her own work could command prices a fraction of those she'd seen, she'd clear enough to keep the shop going for a long time. Will had said the real reason she didn't want her work taken to a gallery was a fear of being made fun of. After some soul-searching, she admitted he was right about that, too.

She felt guilty for the way she'd behaved in Will's office. After all he'd done for her, he didn't deserve to be talked to that way. She'd be sure to contact him before she left to try to make amends—that is, if he would still speak to her. She took another sip of the strong coffee and got some of the foamy milk on the corner of her mouth. As she wiped it away with her napkin, she became aware of someone watching her from the sidewalk.

"I'll bet that's how that old raccoon looked when he scared Judith away from the cabin."

Clem looked up to see Will smiling warily down at her, his eyes as blue as the cloudless sky overhead. She didn't believe she'd ever been as glad to see anyone in her life.

"Elaine told me where you were headed. Can I sit down?"

Clem could only nod. She had so many things to say to him that she didn't know where to start.

"Elaine said you left the jewelry with her—and that you were considering going ahead with the show. I hope you take her up on her offer. You won't be sorry." As a waitress approached the table, Will pointed to Clem's drink and held up two fingers. "I hope this means you believe me now that the show is legitimate."

"Yes, I believe you." Clem looked down at the table a moment before she continued. "I'm sorry I accused you of being dishonest." She looked back up at Will, who reached across the table to take her hand. His touch was firm, strong, reassuring.

"I would never have lied about the show. I may not have been completely straightforward about the loan, that it would be from me and not from a group of investors. But I had the feeling that if you thought the money was coming from me alone, you wouldn't take it."

Clem nodded, acknowledging that this was true.

"And I'm still not sure I'm comfortable taking a personal loan from you."

Will squeezed her hand gently, rubbing the pad of his thumb back and forth across her fingers. "I guess I can understand that. It's a shame, though, because you wrote a helluva business plan."

"Really?"

"Really. I was impressed." Will released her hand when the waitress set their drinks on the table. "Of course, if things at the show go as well as I expect, you'll no longer need a loan from anybody, including me."

Clem took another drink of the warm, rich brew. It tasted twice as good as it had a few minutes ago. "Do you really think so?"

"Absolutely. Elaine thinks so, too, and she knows about these things. If she thinks you're going to be a success, then you are. But as I said, the offer of a loan still stands. In fact, if you were to decide to mass produce and mass market your jewelry, I'd be glad to finance that, too." He took a sip of the steaming coffee and smiled. "But of course, then you'd have to do a new business plan."

"Thanks." Clem was sure she must be glowing. Will liked her business plan, Elaine liked her jewelry, and she had a legitimate art show coming up that could solve her financial problems. She could hardly believe she'd gone through a complete reversal of fortunes since this morning. And the best part was, she had a chance to get back on good terms with Will.

He looked every bit the power broker in his crisp white shirt, burgundy suspenders, and burgundy and navy print tie. He'd left the jacket of his gray suit behind in deference to the heat, and the custom-tailored shirt showed off his shoulders and chest to perfection.

The waitress came back and lingered at Will's side, asking if he had everything he needed. He nodded and gave her a dazzling smile. She wandered away, obviously smitten, and who could blame her? He was a beautiful man. Clem only hoped that what she'd said to him in his office hadn't made him think too badly of her. Her heart skipped a beat when she saw his expression turn serious.

"Now, Clem, about those papers you gave me along with your business plan. How did you come by them?"

Clem explained about the business information service she'd used as a source for the plan, and about where she'd run across the electronic conversation about Will's client company. Will listened, rubbing his chin thoughtfully.

"You did the right thing by giving me that printout. In fact, you may have saved my client millions."

"How?"

"We were working with a client on a deal for a merger with another company. That was what Judith came to the mountains to talk to me about. When the deal reached a critical stage, I had to come back here to take care of things. Then the information you gave us tipped us off to the fact that a third company was about to try a hostile takeover before the merger could take place. Right before I left the office, I put the wheels in motion to thwart the takeover. Without your input, it would have been too late."

Clem stared at him, incredulous. "You mean that I saved your client from a hostile takeover?"

"In a word, yes. It seems that my trusty assistant, Judith, didn't have her finger on the pulse of the industry as much as she claimed. She was completely blindsided by this. But she'll make up for it—she'll have to be the one who does all the grunt work, to make sure everything goes according to plan." A grin spread lazily across Will's face, turning up the corners of his mouth and making his eyes sparkle. "While I finish my vacation."

Will reached across the table again, taking both Clem's hands in his. "Say yes to the show, Clem. And stay with me at least until it's over. I'll show you New York at its best—museums, theater, shopping—you name it."

Clem stared at him, wide-eyed, hardly believing her own ears. "Stay with you at your apartment? I couldn't do that!"

"Why not?"

"It wouldn't be . . . proper."

Will laughed and squeezed her hands, drawing them nearer to him. "Clem, a few days ago we were on a camping trip together, alone in the woods for most of that time. Now, what makes staying with me in my apartment any more improper than that?"

Clem opened her mouth to speak, but could think of no argument to counter this point. In truth, she had begun to worry about where she was going to stay that night. She hadn't a clue as to where to start looking for an affordable hotel. Will began again his sensual massage of her hands. She felt so secure with him. Finally, she said, "All right. But you have to promise to be a gentleman, just like on the camping trip."

Will sighed deeply, either with relief that she'd accepted or with resignation over her condition of acceptance. "I promise to be on my best behavior." He reached for his wallet, laid a bill on the table, and removed another business card, on which he wrote his home address. "I have to go back to the office now and wrap up my part of that deal. After that, I'm all yours. Meet me at the apartment at six o'clock. We'll do a little shopping and then we'll go out and celebrate your show and my business deal. I'll call Elaine and tell her you said yes."

Clem looked at the address—Central Park West. She'd just bet that was a real nice part of town. "I'll be there."

Will grinned broadly and stood up. He took her face in both hands and kissed her lightly, letting his tongue linger over the place where the frothy milk had clung to the corner of her mouth. "We might just have to get a cappuccino machine. I like the way it tastes on you."

Clem whiled away the afternoon in Soho and the Village. She enjoyed visiting other galleries, although she didn't see any she liked as well as Elaine's. She loved the boutiques with their vintage clothing, and even splurged on a string of glass beads at a street market.

As she sat on a bench in the Washington Square park, she decided that Italian ices were almost as good as cappuccino. She believed she could sit and watch New Yorkers all day and not become bored. From the old men playing boccie ball in sandpits to the bagpipe player to the young man walking his pet python, the variety of people and their pursuits was endlessly fascinating.

As she people watched from her bench, her mind returned to her conversation with Will. "I'm all yours," he'd said. A delicious shiver went up her spine that had nothing to do with the icy dessert she was eating. What did he mean when he said he wanted her to stay with him "at least" until the showing?

Later that afternoon Clem took a cab uptown to Will's apartment building, which was almost as tall and not much more inviting than his office building. A dark green awning with the street number sewn in gold script shielded the entrance. Standing pretentiously at parade rest under the awning was a natty doorman. The epaulets on his navy blue uniform were trimmed in the same gold braid as his hat, and his patent leather oxfords were so shiny that Clem was sure she could have seen her reflection in them.

Clem approached him cautiously, wondering if she should know a secret password. "Excuse me," she began. "I'm a friend of Will Fletcher's, and . . ." The look on the doorman's face stopped her before she could finish the sentence. His disapproving gaze swept her from head-to-toe and then leveled on her face as his bushy mustache puffed out like the tail of a scared cat. The expression was such a mixture of cold and comical that she didn't know whether to laugh or run.

"I'm supposed to meet him here at six. Is there a place I could wait?" Clem asked, thinking that there might be an air-conditioned lobby behind the smoky glass door Mr. Mustache was guarding so tenaciously.

Without a word, the doorman raised his arm and pointed across the street. Following the direction of his stubby pointing finger, Clem realized he meant the bench across from them, on the edge of Central Park. "I see," she said coolly. "Be sure to tell Mr. Fletcher where I am, in case he doesn't notice me."

As the doorman eyed her insolently, she thrust out her chin and headed for the park.

"Ooh!" Clem fumed as she collapsed onto the bench, throwing her bag down beside her. A squirrel approached her cautiously. "How do you like that?" Clem asked. "Not even a 'howdy do' or anything."

The squirrel chattered sympathetically.

"You'd think I was a bag lady or something."

Cocking its head to one side, the squirrel hopped closer to Clem's bag.

"Well, just because I've *got* a bag doesn't make me a bag lady." Clem opened the duffle and removed the half-eaten pretzel she'd bought from a street vendor earlier.

She broke off a piece of the doughy bread and tossed it to the squirrel. Clem observed that the passersby looked a good deal different than the residents of the Village. Here the fashions were sophisticated and chic rather than funky and fun. Even the jogging gear looked like designer originals. Clem felt almost as out of place as she had on Wall Street.

The squirrel chattered, asking for another morsel, so Clem tossed it another chunk. It crept closer and sat up on its hind legs. Clem leaned down close to the fuzzy gray creature.

"You're a fearless little fella, I'll say that for you."

"He's a typical New Yorker," came a deep, familiar voice.

Clem looked up at Will, who was standing in front of her, a boyish grin on his face. "We know what we want, and we're not afraid to go after it."

Clem momentarily forgot the squirrel, who made a break for the pretzel, taking it neatly out of her still outstretched hand. "Hey!"

"I think you've just been mugged," Will said, laughing.

"And in broad daylight, too."

"What happened to your famous way with animals?"

"Well, I did have him practically eating out of my hand," Clem said with a feigned pout.

"I'm not impressed. Central Park squirrels will eat out of anybody's hand."

"What can I say? I've been stripped of my magic powers."

Will gave her an appreciative, head-to-toe appraisal. "I don't believe that for a second." He came closer to the bench and picked up her bag, then offered his other hand. "Let's go."

As she took Will's hand a tremor went through her, as it did each time he touched her. With it was the extra thrill of knowing she was going home with him.

Mr. Mustache was considerably warmer toward Clem as she walked up to him hand in hand with Will. He'd been dutifully holding Will's briefcase and suit jacket while Will had gone to fetch her. "Mike, this is Clementine Harper. She's going to be a houseguest of mine. I'm certain you'll take good care of her."

"Of course, Mr. Fletcher," Mike piped up, nodding enthusiastically. Clem would have thought it impossible for the already florid-faced man to get any redder, but Mike flushed to the roots of his hair.

Rather than taking back his belongings, Will hung the strap of Clem's bag over the doorman's arm, the same arm that held the jacket. "Stash our stuff for us, will you? We're going shopping." Clem stifled a giggle. The doorman resembled a human hatrack.

Will took Clem's hand again and led her down to

the next block, where they took the side street, headed west. "Where are we going?"

"To get you a new dress," Will said, loosening his tie. "Tonight we're going out to celebrate your show, and the business deal you helped me with. And as terrific as you look in those jeans, you're going to need something a little dressier where we're going."

Clem's first instinct was to insist that she didn't want to go someplace where she wasn't welcome no matter what she was wearing, but she bit back the remark. After a half hour of watching and comparing herself to the stylish people of this neighborhood, she figured she'd better go along with Will.

After a short walk, they were on Columbus Avenue. "I don't know much about shopping for women's clothes, I'm afraid," Will said, steering them to the right to avoid a baby stroller. "My boss's wife was visiting the office today, and she always looks great, so I asked her if she knew of any nice boutiques around here. Turns out there's one just up the block."

Clem stared at him, aghast, remembering the portraits of the old curmudgeons on the wall outside Will's office. They might be old and sour, but they were also undoubtedly very rich. "Your *boss's* wife? Am I going to be able to afford this place?"

It was Will's turn to stare. "Darling, you won't be paying for this."

Clem stopped in her tracks, rooted to the spot like an obstinant mule. "Whoa. What'd you say?"

Will stood facing her. She could tell by his contrite expression that he knew exactly what he'd said wrong. He drew her closer and put his arm loosely about her shoulders. "Clem, I explained about how you saved my client millions. Now, you're going to need a few things while you're here. I'm going to get them for you, and I want you to think of it as a kind of bonus. Believe me, I would be in big trouble right now if it weren't for your quick thinking." He leaned closer and brushed her brow with a light kiss. "Please let me do this for you."

Clem felt the fight go out of her as his lips skimmed whisper-soft against her skin. She let her head fall onto his shoulder and she felt his cheek, roughened by a five o'clock shadow, against her forehead. After all he had done for her and promised to do for her, the least she could do was try to fit into his world for two weeks. If that meant letting him buy her a couple of outfits, she supposed she could go along with it.

"Okay," she said finally. "But only if they're not too expensive."

"Deal," Will said, giving her shoulder a squeeze.

After a few more minutes' walk, they were standing in front of a glass door lettered with the words:

Dolores Malcolm Fashions:
By Appointment Only.

"Do we have an appointment?"

Will pushed what looked like a doorbell, and a buzzing sound came from somewhere within. "Of course."

Will led her up a steep staircase whose walls were decorated with a tasteful mural of a Parisian street scene. At the top of the stairs a door opened, and a statuesque, sixtyish, blond woman opened the door and motioned them in. "You must be Mr. Fletcher," she said, extending her hand to Will.

"Call me Will, please," he said, shaking her hand. "This is my friend, Clementine Harper."

"What a charming name," Ms. Malcolm enthused.

The woman had a kind face, with plump, rouged cheeks and a ready smile. She was stylishly and taste-fully dressed in a suit tailored to flatter her generous figure. The head-to-toe appraisal Clem braced herself for was subtle, and not insulting. If anything, the woman looked at Clem eagerly, as if she couldn't wait to get started on the transformation.

"Thank you." Clem shook hands with the older woman and looked around. Behind the counter was a seating area with overstuffed Victorian chairs and a loveseat. Mirrors covered two walls, and a curtain led to a back room of some sort.

Mrs. Malcolm invited them to sit, and served them coffee in china cups. "Per your instructions, Will, I've selected some cocktail dresses, evening dresses, and some casual outfits."

Will squeezed Clem's hand as the woman spoke, as if fearing Clem would bolt at the additional ward-robe she mentioned. "Good. Let's get started."

Mrs. Malcolm motioned Clem to follow her. They entered a large room, where she indicated that Clem was to sit at a vanity table. The woman then clasped her hands together and looked at Clem as a sculptor would look at a lump of clay. "Such lovely bone struc-ture," she said. "Don't worry, dear, we're going to make you look like a princess."

Mrs. Malcolm disappeared through a curtain at the back of the room. Clem wondered what Will told the woman about her when he made the appointment. Perhaps he had hinted that the young lady would need some heavy duty help to be made presentable. Or had she drawn her own conclusions about Clem from the way that she was dressed? She probably thought she'd been cast as the fairy godmother in the story of the wealthy but bored young financier philanthropist and the hooker with a heart of gold. Clem shuddered.

Mrs. Malcolm was back in moments, pushing before her a rack of clothing. Clem stood up and looked at the outfits with pleasant surprise. They were stylish but simple, much as she would have chosen herself. Of the three cocktail dresses, Clem's eye went to one immediately. It was a midnight blue sheath ablaze with hundreds of tiny glass beads. "This one." Clem took it off the rack as Mrs. Malcolm cooed her approval.

Clem slipped into one of the dressing rooms and examined the dress for a price tag. Seeing none, she cursed under her breath and slipped into the dress, finding she had to forsake her bra in deference to the skinny straps. She came out of the dressing stall and stepped up to one of the mirrors. The dress fit perfectly. She was surprised at how much she liked herself in it. As she admired the dress, Mrs. Malcolm stepped up behind her and gathered Clem's hair into a twist. Securing it with a rhinestone-encrusted comb, she said, "See how that's done, dear?"

"Yes." Clem had to admit the effect was perfect with the dress.

As if out of thin air, Mrs. Malcolm produced a pair of matching, bead-encrusted pumps. She really was the fairy godmother, Clem thought, slipping them on. Of course they were a perfect fit. "If I get separated from Will, I'll have to leave one of these behind so he can find me again," she whispered to herself, suppressing a giggle at the thought of an investment banker trying shoes on every woman in Manhattan. *When the clock strikes twelve, I'll turn back into a pumpkin—no, a bumpkin.*

"You look lovely, my dear." Mrs. Malcolm beamed. "Shall we model for your gentleman friend?"

The idea of modeling the outfit for Will's approval didn't really thrill her. After all, if she was going to have to wear it, she should make the choice, shouldn't she? It seemed too much like being paraded around like a prize heifer at the county fair. She opened her mouth to decline, but Mrs. Malcolm looked so eager that she didn't have the heart to disappoint her. "Sure, why not?" Clem said gamely.

"Give me a minute." Mrs. Malcolm scurried out of the dressing area and into the room where Will was, the curtain fluttering in her wake. Clem heard her clear her throat in preparation for some kind of fanfare. "May I present, Ms. Clementine Harper."

Clem glanced wistfully behind her at the window facing Columbus Avenue, wishing they weren't on the second floor and wondering how far the jump would be. Sighing, she squared her shoulders and marched out from behind the curtain. Managing what she hoped was a smile, she looked at Will.

For a moment, Will's face registered something like awe, then relaxed into a more controlled expression of masculine appreciation. His gaze raked her from head-to-toe, lingering longer on some parts than others. She fidgeted under the heat of his smoldering scrutiny. Mrs. Malcolm made a circular motion with one arm, indicating that Clem was to turn around. Clem was beginning to feel trapped, and felt herself wishing she was anywhere in the world but there. As she turned, she lost her footing, unaccustomed to the height of the heels she was wearing. She staggered a couple of steps before righting herself.

"You should practice walking in those heels, dear." Mrs. Malcolm clucked solicitously.

Shall I balance a book on my head to improve my posture? Having had all she could take, Clem planted her hands on her hips. "Fashion show's over. Are you going to buy this, or what?"

Mrs. Malcolm looked as if someone had knocked the wind out of her. Will's expression feigned disappointment, but his shoulders shook with silent laughter. "When you put it like that, how can I refuse?" As Clem stalked toward the dressing area, Will called to her, "Don't forget to pick out your dress for the show, and some daytime outfits, too."

Mrs. Malcolm patted Will's shoulder as she hurried after Clem. "You've got a real diamond in the rough there."

Diamonds. He'd like to cover her in diamonds. Will rested his head against the back of the loveseat and closed his eyes. It had been a long, tense, day. Clem's sudden appearance had taken him off guard. Her accusations had shaken him because he'd come so close to losing her, and disturbed him because some of them had come so close to the truth.

He had to be more careful. The woman could smell a lie from fifty paces. It was a miracle he'd found her after she left Elaine's, and made her understand about the loan and the gallery show. Then she'd almost bolted again over the new clothes. He chuckled, wondering how many of the other women he'd dated would turn down the offer of a new wardrobe.

He would have to be more sensitive to her feelings or she would slip through his fingers, like the waters of the mountain stream where he'd first seen her.

Will rubbed his eyes, remembering how she'd

looked sitting in the stream, silvery water swirling around her waist, her wet T-shirt clinging to her breasts, her upturned face full of innocence and promise. His blood surged with warmth and desire.

His original plan had been to lure Clem to New York, to the cold, hard reality of Manhattan, to see if his feelings for her were real—real, and not the product of the mountains and forests, the streams and the campfires, conspiring to help her bewitch him. One look at her, though, her eyes flashing fiery indignation, and he knew he wanted her, mountains or no mountains.

It was said some women were beautiful when they were angry. This one was awesome, devastating, breathtaking. He'd never been so aroused or so terrified as when she stormed into his office. In that moment of crystal awareness, he knew he wanted her as he'd wanted no other woman. He also knew he was on the precipice of losing her. He had two weeks to make her fall in love with him, to make her feel comfortable in a place where she felt she didn't belong. One mistake could rain ruin down around his heart like a firestorm.

There would be no more mistakes. He would maneuver her just like he did the business deals. From now on, this romance would go as smoothly as one of his leveraged buyouts.

"Ain't that just like a man? Sleeping while there's serious shopping to do."

Will's eyes flew open to see Clem staring down at him. He could tell by her quirky grin that she'd recovered at least some of her good humor. Mrs. Malcolm passed them on the way to the counter to total up the charge. Will was on his feet in a flash, steering Clem away from the figures and toward a display of hats in a front corner. "I like this one," he said, jamming a floppy velvet number down over her eyes.

"I can't see," she complained, laughing.

"Just wait. It'll grow on you." Will darted to the counter to sign the charge slip and was back at Clem's side by the time she'd tugged off the makeshift blindfold.

"I don't think so." Clem replaced the hat on the display rack and headed for the counter. By that time Mrs. Malcolm had put away the paperwork and was carefully boxing the clothes with tissue paper.

As Will and Clem left, Mrs. Malcolm called after them, "Have a wonderful evening."

Will took Clem's hand and brought it to his lips for a kiss. "We will. Believe me, we will."

TEN

When they returned to Will's apartment building laden with packages, the doorman held the door open for them, deferentially doffing his gold-trimmed hat to Clem with a smile.

Will led her through a small but sumptuously decorated lobby and into an elevator. He placed a key into a slot on the elevator's control panel and turned it. Seconds later, the doors opened—not into a hallway, as Clem had expected, but into the foyer of Will's apartment.

"Wow, I've only ever seen that in the movies," Clem exclaimed, standing stock-still.

"What's that?"

"Where an elevator opens out right into someone's apartment."

"There are advantages and disadvantages to that arrangement. The bad part of it is that if you forget to step off the elevator you will eventually go back down again." Will reached out a hand for her.

"Oh, yeah." She took his hand and finally walked out into the foyer. Will led her from the foyer into the living area.

The apartment's living room was furnished in modern style, probably by a professional decorator, she guessed. The carpet, chairs, and sofas were off-white. Chrome and glass coffee and end tables held a book here, an unobtrusive *objet d'art* there. A few paintings provided muted splashes of color.

Overall, Clem mentally summed up the decor as tasteful, elegant, and cold. She felt disappointed, somehow. She supposed she'd hoped Will's apartment would seem warm and welcoming, a refuge from the city streets. Instead it felt lifeless and uninviting. "Nice place you have here." She was pretty sure she managed to smile.

"Thanks," Will said, grinning. "Let's get all this later." He took Clem's packages from her and set them next to the ones he'd been carrying. His briefcase and her duffle were sitting there too, having been brought up earlier by Mike the doorman. "I want to show you around."

Will gave her a tour of the apartment, including the state-of-the art kitchen and exquisitely appointed dining room. As they walked down the hall to the bedrooms, Clem felt a prickle of anxiety in her stomach. She was about to learn what the sleeping arrangements were. Did he intend to honor his promise to be a gentleman?

"This is the master bedroom." He opened a door and flicked on the light. The room was somewhat more inviting than the rest of the apartment. It was decorated in earth tones with a southwestern flavor and oak furniture. The bed was huge. Would he expect her to share it with him?

He made no attempt to draw her inside, but proceeded to the next bedroom. "And this is your room." He pushed open that door to reveal a nondescript guest room with a bed, chest of drawers, desk, nightstand, and a couple of chairs. Clem let out a sigh of relief. She *did* have her own room, and she found its simplicity comforting. Will pointed to a door on the far wall. "The bathroom, dressing room, and walk-in closet are through that door, if you'd like to freshen up and change before we go out to dinner."

After Clem had put her new outfits in the closet and unpacked her duffle, she drew a bath and sank into the steamy, lavender-scented water. She had no idea how tired she was until her muscles responded to the delicious heat. She still hadn't recovered from the long, cramped bus trip. Soon, though, she began to relax.

She'd found the bathroom stocked with various toiletries such as bath oil and shampoo. He was either a very thoughtful host, or the items had been left by the last guest. She wondered with a pang of jealousy how many female houseguests he'd had. What was she thinking? Most of them probably stayed with him in *his* room. She thought of his bedroom, easily the most inviting room in the apartment, and sank lower in the tub, letting the water rise to her chin. With her leaving in two weeks, a physical relationship with Will would only complicate her life, and goodness knew it was complicated enough already. The events of today alone were enough to make her head spin.

After her bath she dressed carefully in the new cocktail dress and dried her hair. Mrs. Malcolm, whose watchword was "accessorize," had thoughtfully provided lingerie, hosiery, an evening bag, and even some makeup samples. She'd also insisted that Clem take the rhinestone comb. Clem applied the makeup and recreated the hairstyle as best she could. Tucking a few things into the evening bag, she surveyed the results in the mirror. She guessed she could pass for a sophisticate as long as she kept her mouth shut. "You can take the girl out of the country, but you can't take the country out of the girl," she muttered to her reflection.

As Clem walked into the living room, it was her turn to be awestruck. Will wore a tuxedo—wore it to perfection, as if he'd just stepped off the cover of *GQ*. His wavy hair was tamed into onyx-black sleekness. His snow-white evening shirt emphasized his deep tan.

They drew closer together as they appraised each other. "You look beautiful," he said.

"You're not so bad yourself, city boy."

Will reached out for her as if about to pull her into his arms, but stopped and only massaged her shoulders gently. "Let's go."

Once outside, Will led Clem to a waiting limo. The uniformed driver opened the door and Clem slipped inside, marvelling at how big the interior was. Will sat down beside her, and they were off into the Manhattan night. As they crossed over to Fifth Avenue to make their way south, Will pointed out places of interest, but Clem was more interested in what was inside the limo. "I can't believe there's a TV in here. And liquor." Clem pointed to the row of decanters in a side pocket.

Will laughed. "Would you like a drink?"

"Oh, no. I'm not much of a drinker. Don't like the taste of the stuff."

"How about a nice glass of wine when we get to the restaurant?"

"Hmm, I don't know. I'm not that fond of wine, either." Clem was too embarrassed to admit that she'd never actually had any wine that came from a bottle with a cork in it. The wine that uncle Jess made tasted more like pancake syrup than anything else.

"I just might be able to pick out some wine you'll like," Will said, slipping his arm around her shoulders and drawing her close.

They reached the restaurant in minutes. Clem had her door halfway open before the driver had a chance to open it for her. "Oops, I forgot. You're supposed to wait for him to open the door, aren't you?"

"That's quite all right," Will said. "I always thought having the door opened for you was a strange custom, anyway. I mean, we're able-bodied people, aren't we?"

Some of us are more able-bodied than others, Clem thought as his rock-hard thigh touched hers. Inside, a short foyer led to a sumptuous dining room. In the center of the room was a black marble fountain. Above it was a chandelier that was at least six feet across. Mesmerized by the thousands of tiny crystals dancing in the light, Clem stared at it, blinking, until Will gently took her elbow. "You're going to see spots before your eyes if you're not careful."

A pear-shaped little man who looked for all the world like a penguin in his maître d' regalia stared at her with an expression of tolerant disdain. Clem sighed. Not thirty seconds into the front door, and they'd already made her for a hick. When he had her attention, he did a crisp about-face and walked away. "We're supposed to follow him," Will whispered pleasantly.

Clem strode forward, trying to keep up with the maître d' without tripping on her high heels. The man stopped at a table for two on the far side of the room and pulled one of the chairs away from the table. Clem

sat down, followed by Will. Then the man gave them
menus and a wine list, and was gone. "I don't think
he likes me," confided Clem. "I was afraid to sit down
for fear he would jerk the chair out from under me."

Clem relaxed a little at the sound of Will's deep
laughter. He stared, as if the sight of her satisfied a
hunger, a craving that could not be sated by anything
he might find on the restaurant's menu. Clem felt a
flush of warmth rise to her cheeks and picked up her
menu, raising it in front of her face. "What's good
here?" she asked, trying to sound casual.

"Everything," he said simply, still staring.

A man carrying a water pitcher wrapped in linen
introduced himself as Jean, their waiter. Clem listened as he rattled off the chef's recommendations,
mostly in French. With a subtle bow, the waiter left,
and another man appeared at Will's elbow. Without
looking at the wine list, Will gave the man a long,
French-sounding name Clem had never heard before.

"Very *well*, sir," said the young man, looking clearly
pleased, and he hurried away.

"Need any help with the menu?" Will offered.

"Yes, if you don't mind. My high school French is
a little rusty," Clem admitted. She'd also probably
need help with the flatware. There was such a variety
of knives, forks, and spoons that she had no idea
which to use when. The idea struck her that if she
ordered the exact same thing as Will, she could follow his lead. "So what are you having?" she asked.

"I'm having the prime rib. It's very good here, especially for a French place."

"Well, then, I'll just have it, too."

"Are you sure? I'd be glad to go over the rest of

the menu with you. I want to make sure you order something you'll really like."

"Sure, I'm sure." Clem sipped her water to soothe her throat, which was becoming dry, as it always did when she was nervous. "Do you come here often?" *And with whom?* she wondered.

"Every now and then. But only on special occasions." His eyes glittered.

There was something about the light that made his eyes look the bluest blue Clem had ever seen. And she thought she'd been dazzled by the chandelier!

The wine steward appeared again with the bottle of wine and a silver ice bucket. He poured a bit of the ruby-colored liquid into Will's glass and waited for his appraisal. Will swirled the wine, tasted it, and nodded. The steward poured Clem's wine and refilled Will's glass. Then he settled the bottle in the ice bucket and was gone.

Will raised his glass, leaning forward. "To a very special woman, who I predict is on the verge of a brand new life."

"Hmm. That's a strong statement." Clem brought the wine to her lips. She took a sip, lost her breath, and coughed, covering her mouth with her napkin.

"Are you all right?" Will seemed ready to spring from his seat to come to her aid if necessary.

"I have to be honest with you," Clem said, recovering her breath. "All wine tastes like vinegar to me. Cheap or expensive, it's all the same. I'm afraid your nice bottle of wine is wasted on me. I'm sorry. I know you wanted me to like it."

Clem had the feeling she'd just flunked some kind of litmus test of whether she could be sophisticated— kind of like the princess and the pea, only instead of a legume and a stack of mattresses, her test had involved fermented grape juice.

"Don't apologize." Will smiled his good-natured, understanding smile. "We'll just keep trying until we find something you do like."

After Will gave their order to Jean the waiter, he beckoned to the wine steward once more and pointed to an item on the wine list. After the steward scurried away again, Will said, "Would you like to dance?"

"Sure."

With some trepidation, Clem let Will lead her to the dance floor. She didn't feel like a competent dancer even when she wasn't wearing what felt like eight-inch heels. But when Will drew her close to him, she ceased to worry about her dancing ability. All she could think about was how good it felt to be close to him, swaying to the music in the circle of his arms. She closed her eyes, breathing in his clean, masculine scent, and involuntarily tightened her grip on his shoulder.

When she laid her cheek against his chest, she found she could hear his heart beating. That intimate sound sent a ripple of contentment through her, and she sighed. She felt him take a deep breath and hug her tighter. He murmured something she couldn't hear, except for two words—"Wild child."

His old endearment for her seemed strange now. So much had happened to her since he'd uttered it last. Only a few hours ago, she had gotten off a bus, scared and alone, with nothing but a few belongings in a duffle bag. Now, dressed to the nines, she was in the arms of a powerful and attractive man, dancing in an elegant ballroom. She felt like Cinderella at the ball.

Her mind returned to the last time she'd heard him use his pet name for her. It had been at his cabin. *How do you tame a wild child?* he had said. Her eyes flew open, and the sound of Will's heartbeat was drowned out by the ring of the remembered words in her ears. How *would* you tame a wild child? First, lure her to New York, get her some new clothes and makeup, and start schooling her in the finer things— wine, fancy restaurants, limousines. . . . The thought made her wince. She knew Will liked her, but did he like her the way she was, or was he hoping to mold her into something else? Some*one* else?

Suddenly, she realized Will wasn't moving anymore. She looked up, blinking, into blue velvet eyes. The music had stopped, and they were the only ones on the dance floor. She stepped away from him, glancing around self-consciously to see if anyone was staring. "Sorry. I didn't notice the music had stopped," she whispered.

"Don't be. Neither did I."

As Will led her back to their table, Clem resolved to put her disconcerting thoughts behind her and enjoy the evening. Will had done some very nice things for her today, and she would not question his motives—at least, not until he had given her a reason.

The wine steward was waiting with yet another bottle. As they took their seats he removed the cork, and there was a loud "pop." He poured the gently sparkling liquid into two crystal glasses and settled the bottle into the ice bucket beside the first one.

"For an occasion like this, I should have ordered champagne from the beginning. But better late than never, eh? See if you like this better than the wine."

Clem was skeptical, but gamely picked up the glass. As soon as she'd brought it to mouth level, the tiny bubbles tickled her nose oh so slightly, and she laughed. Tentatively, she sipped, and a delightful taste filled her mouth. This was wonderful. "I love it!"

Will smiled with satisfaction. "I knew you would. Champagne suits you."

"Why? Because I'm bubbly and sweet? I don't think so," Clem said between sips.

Will set down his glass and raked her with a thirsty look. "Because you're intoxicating."

Clem felt warmth spread through her body, and it wasn't from the effects of the champagne. She wished she could think of something witty to say, but her mind went blank as she stared into those mesmerizing eyes.

The waiter appeared as if by magic, and she silently thanked him for his timing. As the hearty aroma of the food reached her nose, she realized just how hungry she was. She spread her napkin across her lap and waited for Will to begin, but he appeared to be waiting for her. Looking at the array of silverware, Clem shrugged. How could she go wrong with a knife and fork? She picked hers up and tasted the prime rib. It was even better than it smelled.

Will refilled her glass as he explained more about the business deal that she had, by chance, helped him with. She didn't really understand the particulars, and her mind wandered. She found she was still worried about what was to come. How awkward was it going to be to stay in Will's apartment and keep their relationship uncomplicated by lovemaking? On the one hand, she felt as if she should take this opportunity to establish some ground rules, but on the other, he had made it clear that she had her own room. He had promised to behave like a gentleman.

Only thing was, tonight he was behaving like a gentleman trying to win a woman's heart—and he was succeeding.

She took another drink of champagne. The stuff just seemed to get better and better. In addition to making her head light and her arms and legs heavy, the champagne seemed to be making her companion more charming and handsome as the night progressed. Who was she kidding? She wasn't really that concerned that Will would lose control. It was her own control that she was worried about.

"More champagne?" Will reached for the bottle.

"No, thanks." Clem hoped that wasn't a slur in her voice she'd heard. "If I drink anymore, I'll be seeing double." One Will was devastating enough. Two would be more than she could stand. She giggled at the thought, and clapped her hand over her mouth.

"Don't do that." Will smiled and reached for her hand, gently pulling it away from her face and toward his. "I love it when you giggle." He kissed her fingers gently before releasing her hand. The small gesture touched Clem deeply. In this small way he had encouraged her to be herself. Perhaps she should assert her identity a little more, just to gauge his reaction.

Jean the waiter materialized. "Was everything to your satisfaction?"

Clem dabbed at her mouth with the linen napkin. "John, that was some mighty fine eatin'."

Jean's eyebrows raised. "Thank you. I'll tell the chef. He'll be so pleased."

Clem looked at Will, whose shoulders were shaking almost imperceptibly with suppressed laughter. She'd amused him, but hadn't embarrassed him. That was a good sign.

After another dance and a leisurely dessert and

coffee, Clem and Will left the restaurant and got into the limo for the trip back to Will's apartment. "I think you should practice walking on those high heels before you wear them again," Will teased. "I was afraid you were going to fall into the fountain on the way out."

"Forget the heels. What I need to practice is drinking half a bottle of champagne."

When they got out of the limo, Will took her hand and started to lead her under the awning of the apartment building, but Clem hung back. Will noticed that she was peering straight up at the sky. "What is it?" he asked, following her gaze. "Does champagne make you see flying saucers, or something? I don't see a thing."

Clem didn't laugh at his joke. "I can't see the stars. The city lights are too bright." A strange sadness gripped her.

"Come with me. I'll show you something that's just as good as the stars."

Back in Will's apartment, Clem felt the tension creeping back into her chest. Would he kiss her? They'd just returned from a date, after all. Only instead of being on her doorstep, where dates usually ended up, they were in his apartment. It was literally a sobering thought. Clem thought she felt the effects of the champagne evaporating.

"Come here." Will did not turn on a light, but took her hand and led her deeper into the dark apartment.

Uh-oh, Clem thought.

Will reached for something, presumably a light switch, and the heavy drapes that covered the outer wall began to part. The entire wall of the apartment was glass. She was looking out onto Manhattan at midnight. It was breathtaking. Central Park sprawled beneath them. Beyond it were the skyscrapers, lit up in all their nighttime glory.

"What do you think?"

Clem looked at Will. He wasn't looking at the skyline at all, but at her, as if trying to see it all through her eyes instead of his own.

"It's magnificent," she said reverently.

"Not nearly as magnificent as you." Will put his arms around her and drew her close to him. He brought his lips down on hers, gently at first, then with more urgency, forcing her lips apart, tasting her. One hand explored her back while the other found the rhinestone comb and removed it, freeing her hair.

He cupped her bottom, molding her to him, and she felt his need for her. Then she felt her own need, burning low in her body and spiraling outward. She returned the kiss, encircling his neck with one arm and caressing his shoulder with the other hand. She delighted in the feel of his iron bicep underneath his crisp evening shirt.

Just as she thought she was about to become lost in his kiss, she felt him begin to release her. As he eased her away from him, he looked down at her. His hooded eyes were filled with emotion. Why had he stopped? She wondered, blinking up at him.

As if reading the silent question in her thoughts, he said, "I don't want to go back on my word to behave like a gentleman. Not so soon, anyway." He managed a grin. His eyes captured the moonlight and shone a deep, dark, ocean blue.

Will let go of her arms as one would let go of a toddler just beginning to walk. She hadn't been aware of how much she was tottering on the high heels, how close she'd come to swooning in his embrace. She righted herself and stood straight. "Good. Good. I'm glad."

Disoriented and not knowing what else to do, Clem turned toward her bedroom, then remembered her manners. "Thank you, Will. I had a lovely evening. I'll never forget it."

Will turned on a light for her and loosened his tie. "You're welcome. Neither will I."

As Clem disappeared down the hallway, Will released a pent-up breath. He braced himself with one hand against the glass and hung his head, his body slumping in an attitude of weariness. It had taken all his strength to break off the kiss, every ounce of his will not to carry Clem to his bedroom and make love to her.

His gaze came to rest on the rhinestone comb he had dropped carelessly on the carpet. He picked it up and stroked it, holding it up to the light. Groaning, he leaned against the wall again, pressing his flushed cheek to the glass, hoping its coolness would calm what felt like fever. He was on fire for her, but he couldn't seduce her yet. It was too soon. If he came on too strong now, she'd run. Run like the rabbit in her dream.

He would use the next week to make her fall in love with him—and with New York. When the time was right, she'd be his. She'd stay.

A week later, Clem sat on a bench in the Museum of Natural History and observed a group of schoolchildren clustered around an exhibit about Native American culture. She smiled at the youngsters as they stared in awe at the huge canoe and the Indians it bore. The Indians were only mannequins, of course, but as far as Clem could tell from their dress, they were accurate representations of Native Americans.

Of all the sights she had seen the last week, this museum was her favorite. The Native American exhibits fascinated her because of her own heritage, and the collection of gemstones was so fabulous that she could have stood and stared at those exhibits for hours. She'd decided to visit the museum again this afternoon, when Will had said he had to take care of some business matters. He'd said he would meet her here before closing time, and take her to a place she'd really like.

Clem leaned back and closed her eyes. She was tired, but it was a good kind of tired. The last week had been like a beautiful dream—not to mention a whirlwind of activity. Will had taken her to every imaginable place he thought she would enjoy, and she had loved them all. They'd seen several Broadway shows, which she'd adored—especially the musicals—except that the crowds made her nervous. They'd toured every major art museum in the city, where she'd been awestruck by actually seeing so many of the original works she had only read about in books.

He took her on tours of many of New York's distinctive neighborhoods like Chinatown and Little Italy, where the food was fabulous and the people endlessly fascinating. Will had even taken her on a private, candlelight dinner cruise around Manhattan, complete with violins and roses.

And the shopping. He'd completely worn down her resistance when it came to letting him buy her gifts. She had protested his continuing to buy her presents so strongly that they had had to reach a compromise. She'd agreed to let him buy her things only if they were inexpensive. After that, he'd made quite a show of buying her the cheapest, tackiest souvenirs imaginable, sending her into gales of laughter whenever he presented her with one. She had such an extensive collection of them that she had no idea how she would get them back home.

Home. A wave of homesickness went over her, like a dark cloud chased by a bitter wind. She missed her mountains so. She both longed for and dreaded the day when she could go back home. It would be the day she returned to the life she loved, but also the day she'd leave Will forever. Her worst fear had come true. She was falling in love with him. He had been so kind and loving to her the last week. And best of all, he had treated her with respect. He hadn't expected anything in return for his kindness, which made her want to give him everything. After the giving, though, when she left him, she'd leave a piece of her heart behind.

Will entered the museum and saw Clem on the marble bench, looking for all the world as if she'd fallen asleep. How could anyone fall asleep in the midst of the din being made by dozens of children, all chattering at once? He approached her slowly, fascinated by watching her sleep. How he'd love to watch this angel sleeping in his bed, he thought. She must have been worn out by all the activity of the last week. Not too worn out, he hoped.

It had surprised him how much he'd enjoyed the last week with Clem, platonic though it was. He hadn't realized how jaded he'd become about his life and surroundings. Her enthusiasm for each new adventure was so infectious. It was almost as if he saw things through her eyes—for the first time. He'd never forget the expression on her face when the curtain went up on her first Broadway musical. How her eyes filled with awe as she first laid eyes on paintings in the Metropolitan Museum of Art. Her whoop of delight when she first entered Yankee stadium. Her breathless wonder at the sounds of her first opera.

The week had been intoxicating, and he hadn't even laid a hand on her. When he did finally get her to his bed, he feared he might die of happiness. It would be soon now. Very soon. Darkness would be here in only a couple of hours. Then he would show her an evening he hoped neither of them would ever forget.

As he came closer, he froze. A look of sorrow crossed her face, so profound that it caused an involuntary pang of sympathetic pain in Will's own chest and filled him with a sense of foreboding. He closed the rest of the distance between them on three long strides and put a hand gently on her shoulder.

"Hey there, sleeping beauty. What's wrong? Were you having another nightmare?" He put his hand on her forehead and smoothed back her hair.

She smiled up at him and sighed. "I wasn't asleep, just daydreaming."

Will frowned. "Most people daydream about good things. From the look on your face, I'd say—"

Clem put her fingertips to his lips. "Shhh. Let's not talk about it."

Will covered her hand with his own, pressing her fingers harder to his lips, kissing them. He couldn't stand the thought that she was troubled about anything. It was ridiculous, he knew, to think that he could wave a wand and make everything perfect for a person as complex as Clem, but that's just what he wanted to do. Would what he had in store for her tonight quell her doubts and fears, or simply add to them? His plan would work. It had to.

"I have a great idea. We have a couple of hours before dinner. Let's go shopping."

Clem gave him a look of exasperation. "Will, you've bought me too much stuff already. I was just sitting here wondering how I'm going to get it all home with me."

Will managed a grin, hoping that his face didn't betray the pang he felt, hearing her speak of leaving. "Whatever I buy you will be small. I promise."

Clem shrugged and allowed Will to pull her to her feet. Once outside, he said, "Where we're going isn't far, but since you're tired, why don't we ride instead of walk?"

"I don't mind walking, really."

Will led her toward a waiting hansom cab. *She'll love this,* he thought. He walked to the step of the carriage to help her up into the seat, but instead of following him she walked directly to the horse, frowning. When Will joined her, she was stroking the horse's nose and peering into its liquid black eyes. The animal had a dignified but melancholy air about him, and responded to her touch by nuzzling her gently.

"Clem, are you ready to go?"

"He's not happy."

Will saw the grim set of Clem's jaw and the fervent light in her eyes and felt his body go tense in anticipation—of what, he didn't know. He decided to try and lighten the mood. "Why shouldn't he be happy? He's got a good steady job, nice shoes. . . ." Her withering glare cut him off.

"He should be in a pasture somewhere breathing clean air instead of pounding the pavement, inhaling exhaust fumes, and wearing blinders."

Will scratched his head. "Well, so should we all, when you think about it."

"Do you want a ride, or not?" called the driver, clearly annoyed.

"Not!"

Will saw Clem's face register defiance, indecision, helplessness, and finally resignation. It was the helplessness that made his chest tighten. Her bottom lip quivered as she bent forward and kissed the horse's velvety nose. "I'm sorry, baby. I can't help you."

Clem stormed off down the sidewalk at a pace that forced Will to jog to catch up with her. "I'll buy you the horse. We can put him out to pasture in some farm upstate somewhere, if you want."

The fears he'd just experienced in the museum hit him full force. Making Clem happy, the thing he wanted to do most in the world, would not always be as easy as taking her to a show or buying her a trinket here and there. The things that seemed to satisfy other women would not always satisfy Clem. The thought thrilled him, yet made him uneasy.

Clem wheeled on him. "Is that your solution to every problem? To throw money at it? You can't buy all the hansom cab horses!"

Will gave her a skeptical look.

"Okay. Okay, so you *can*. But you won't, because it wouldn't do any good. There would only be more to take their places." Clem flung her hands out in exasperation. "Will, you can't fix this."

He stood speechless. He'd accepted that she could read the minds of animals, as she had with the horse. Now she was reading his mind. His conviction that he could make everything perfect for her, which had been so much on his mind, was wrong. That realization frightened him. He was a man who liked to be in control, and with Clem he could never be certain that he was.

Standing there on the sidewalk in the late afternoon sun, he looked at Clem. There was fire in her eyes, and her cheeks were flushed with emotion, just as they were when she'd come to his office that day— the day she'd come to get her jewelry back, furious that he had taken it upon himself to sell it for her. It suddenly hit him—what had been so obvious from the beginning. If Clem were to fall in love with him, it would be for the person he was, not for his ability to give her a perfect world, a perfect life—because there was no such thing.

Fear had never been in his repertoire of emotions. In fact, he'd built a career and a reputation on fearlessness. Looking at Clem now, though, he was afraid, afraid for the first time in his life that he wouldn't measure up. His money and power meant nothing to her. All he could offer her was himself. Would that be enough? He'd have to start back to work soon, and he wouldn't be able to spend as much time with her as he had been. Even if tonight went the way he wanted it to, would he be able to keep her with him? It wasn't often that his self-confidence faltered, and he didn't like the feeling.

"You're right." Will swallowed hard. "I can't fix this. But if I could, I would. I would do anything in the world for you. You know that, don't you?"

Clem sighed, and looked at the sidewalk. "Yes. I know you would. You've been so good to me, but you can't change the city into the country. You can't put soft grass under the feet of a horse who pounds the hot pavement for his food and shelter, you can't house all the homeless people, and you can't bring out the stars."

Will walked up to her and put his arms around her shoulders. "You're right. Except for the part about the stars. I wouldn't be so sure about that if I were you."

Clem laughed gently and her expression softened. "I'll believe it when I see it. Rising on tiptoe, she kissed him on the cheek. "Thanks for trying, though."

As they walked away arm-in-arm, Will thought about his plans for tonight. No longer as confident as he had been, he began to think about the possible downside. The flaw in his plan was that it might actually have the opposite effect from what he wanted. Clem had been responding so wonderfully to him. He couldn't bear the thought that a miscalculation on his part might frighten her away from him. Tonight would take all the tenderness and sensitivity he could muster, two qualities that he'd never thought he possessed until Clem had come along and brought out the best in him.

Still, his instincts told him the time was right to deepen their relationship and make a proposal that would change both their lives—if it didn't drive her away first.

ELEVEN

Clem wound up the music box that Will had bought her that afternoon at FAO Schwarz and set it down on the dresser in her bedroom. A tiny prince and princess danced to "Lara's Theme" from *Dr. Zhivago*, safe and secure in their perfect world under a glass dome. She sighed. If only real life could be so simple.

She checked her reflection once more as the final, fragile notes from the music box slowed and then died away. Will had asked her to wear the dress she wore on their first night out. He seemed to love that dress on her, so he must be taking her someplace special. She applied her lipstick and went to join him in the living room.

He was wearing his tuxedo again, with one difference—this time he wore a small, white boutonniere. He held a box in his hand, which he opened as she came closer. His smile was more dazzling than she'd ever seen it. "This is for you." He removed a perfect white orchid.

He began to pin the corsage on her, but he stopped, poised in mid-air, when he realized there was no discreet way to do so. Also, was it her imagination, or were his hands shaking ever so slightly? Surely not.

The dress's tiny spaghetti straps left no real place on which to anchor the thing, and below that, well, that was dangerous territory. They both laughed.

"Here, let me," Clem offered, pausing to savor its sweet fragrance before deftly pinning the corsage to the very top of the dress.

"Thanks."

"No. Thank *you*. It's lovely. We must be going someplace special."

"Oh, we are."

He led her into the elevator, but instead of pushing the button for the lobby he inserted his key in the control panel and touched a different button.

"What are you up to?"

"Wait and see." Will grinned rakishly. He leaned toward her and closed his eyes. "You smell heavenly tonight. I'll bet even angels don't smell as good as you."

Clem blushed. "It's the corsage."

Will shook his head. The elevator stopped, and they stepped out onto the roof. Clem blinked to clear her vision. She couldn't be seeing what she thought she was. After a moment she realized that what seemed to be hundreds of twinkling stars were actually hundreds of tiny white Christmas lights strung randomly overhead and covering dozens of potted trees. She felt as if she were in the middle of an enchanted forest in a fairy tale.

In the center of the little copse of trees was an elegant table set for two with fine linen, silver, crystal, and an ice bucket with chilling champagne. A candle flickered in its silver holder beside a vase with a single red rose.

To one side was a tent, not the kind Clem was used to but a fancy green-and-white striped tent with tassels on the corners. It looked to Clem like the tents she had seen in movies about dashing desert sheiks and their harems. The flap was fastened back with a piece of gold braid, to reveal an elegant, chintz-covered sofa in a coordinating fabric. At each side of the sofa was an end table with its own vase of long-stemmed red roses.

"Don't tell me," Clem said. "Let me guess. You wanted me to feel at home, so you pitched me a tent."

"You got it. Only this is camping Manhattan style." Will took her hand and led her to the table. "Would you like some champagne?"

She arched an eyebrow.

"That was an awfully silly question, wasn't it? Of course you would." He laughed.

Clem laughed, too, as Will uncorked the bottle. He poured a glass and handed it to her, then filled his own. "A toast," he said, holding up his glass. "To us."

"Ooh." Clem clinked her glass against his as a ripple of excitement went through her. What did he mean? She had a feeling she would soon find out. She took a sip of the sparkling liquid. Maybe it would calm her nerves, but she doubted it. She got a funny humming feeling in her stomach, and it wasn't from the champagne. Will had said it was going to be a special night. She knew she was about to find out what he'd meant.

Will stepped into the shadows next to the elevator door and music began to drift through the air like a sweet fragrance. It was jazz—slow, laid-back and sensuous. Music to make love by.

Clem's next sip of champagne was more like a gulp.

Will took her empty glass and set it down on the table along with his. "Let's dance."

She'd danced with him many times over the last week. Tonight, in the privacy of their rooftop paradise, there were no prying eyes of other diners. They both felt the freedom their isolation afforded. Clem wrapped both arms around Will's neck, stroking his silky hair where it curled just a bit at his collar. He flattened her body against his own, boldly spreading his hand over her bottom. His other hand wrapped all the way around her back, until his fingertips touched the side of her breast.

When the tape stopped their bodies continued to sway, rocking gently to no other music but the feel of each other. Finally, Clem raised her head from his chest and looked up at him. "I can't believe you've done all this for me. I can't believe this whole past week. I've had a wonderful time. It's all been like magic."

Will stroked her back in small circles, like in a massage. "It's been like that for me, too."

His eyes locked on hers with a look so intense she had to look away. Her gaze traveled back to the strings of lights crisscrossing overhead. "I love the lights. But you shouldn't have gone to such trouble."

"I knew you were disappointed when you looked up the other night and you couldn't see the stars for the city lights." Will put his hand to her face, cupping it and bringing her gaze to his once more. "I wanted to give them back to you. I wanted to give you the stars."

Tears came to Clem's eyes. She tightened her arms

around his neck and pressed her face to his chest. "Thank you."

"What's this?" Will whispered, gently stroking her hair, a look of concern creasing his brow. "I thought you said you were having a wonderful time."

"I am. It's just that, well, the gallery show's a week from tonight. And then I'll have to go back home. And . . . and I'll miss you, so much." Clem resolved that she wouldn't break down completely, no matter how wretched she felt. Sniffling, she pulled away from Will and wiped at her cheeks with her palms. "I started dreading having to leave practically from our first evening together."

Will produced his handkerchief and patted her face with it. "I feel the same way. That's what I brought you here to talk about."

Through the haze of her tears, Clem saw him smile. He led her into the tent and sat on the sofa, pulling her down beside him. He took both her hands in his and fixed his bluer-than-blue eyes on hers. "I want you to stay here with me."

"What? I can't do that." Clem looked at him in alarm, her heart lurching. The knowledge that he wanted her with him almost made her weep—for joy and the pain of loss at the same time. "I have to go back to the mountains. This isn't where I belong. I'd go crazy living here."

Will gripped her hands tighter and brought his face close to hers. "You just said yourself that you've had a wonderful time here this past week. Clem, we could have a wonderful life if you'd just give it a chance."

A wonderful life? Trembling with emotion, Clem tried to pull herself together. She had to think clearly. "You're right. I have been happy the past week. Because you've been with me every minute, making things perfect for me. But Monday morning you go back to work, and I'm on my own. What then?"

She saw a cloud of doubt pass over Will's face. "You'll be fine. It's safe for you to go anywhere you want in the daytime while I'm at work. And at night, when I get home, we can be together like we have been." A sensuous grin played at the corners of his mouth. "Only I hope you won't make me promise to behave like a gentleman forever."

"I don't know." Clem bit her lip. She'd never faced a more agonizing decision. And the hell of it was, she knew she'd be unhappy either way. She could either have Will and be cooped up in a concrete and steel prison, or she could have her mountains and the carefree lifestyle she loved, and lose him.

Will put his arm around her shoulders and twined his fingers in her hair. "Clem, you said earlier that you don't belong here. That's not true. You belong with me. Promise me that you'll think about what I've said over the next week. You can give me your answer after the show."

Clem nodded and relaxed against his shoulder. He freed his hand from her hair and reached around to stroke her cheek, guiding her face to his. Pressing his lips to hers, he gathered her closer. His hand caressed her hip and then began a downward descent, gathering the material of her dress as it went in search of her thigh.

His kiss deepened as he claimed her mouth again and again. She gasped for air as his lips left hers and blazed a slow trail down her throat. His touch was igniting her body and clouding her mind. In the midst of the smoldering haze of sensation that was building within her, she made a decision. She put her hands against his chest and pushed gently but firmly until he loosened his grip on her.

He leaned back, his face flushed and his eyes black with desire. His breath came fast and hard, and the look on his face tugged at her heart even though she knew what was going to come next. She stood up and took two steps back from the sofa.

"Clem," Will began hoarsely. "If you want our relationship to stay platonic during the next week when you're making up your mind, it's all right with me. I'm a man. You know what I want. But if you're not sure of what *you* want, I'm going to give you all the time you need. That's how much I care about you."

Clem smiled down at him. "You're going to give me all the time I need, are you?" She put her hands underneath her hair and lifted it across one shoulder. "Well, just for that . . ." Reaching behind her, she slowly unzipped her dress. "I'm going to give *you* the stars."

Will made no attempt to disguise the desire in his eyes, and Clem savored it. She soon stood on the sequined puddle that was her cocktail dress. Lifting the dress gently with the toe of her shoe, she set it aside so as not to damage the corsage. Then she slowly stepped out of her lacy slip.

Will's gaze followed her every move. He felt hypnotized—it was like the incredible feeling she'd given him in the mountains, performing her bird pantomime in front of the campfire. This was no sleight of hand, though. It was a deeper, almost otherworldly feeling. One thought penetrated his almost intoxicated mental state: *She was about to be his.*

The strapless slip followed the dress to the floor. Her tanned legs allowed her to go without pantyhose in the summer, as she preferred, and the dress's tiny

straps made wearing a bra impossible. So she stood
before him in only a bit of lace and a pair of high-
heeled snakeskin pumps. Seductively, she bit her bottom lip, and he understood instinctively that she was
going to know exactly how to please him. He gasped,
having for the last few moments forgotten to breathe.

He felt compelled to say something profound, but
words failed him. He heard himself say only, "You're
beautiful," a statement woefully inadequate to de-
scribe what he saw before him. She stepped within
his reach and he took her by the waist, drawing her
toward him. He wanted to stand, but found he could
not. The strength had gone from his legs, but fortu-
nately seemed to have settled in a nearby part of his
body. He pressed his face to her belly, planting kisses
there and reaching upward to cup her breasts.

She ran her fingers through his hair and linked
them together at the back of his head, pressing him
closer to her. He pulled her down onto his knee. She
moaned, feeling his arousal, and he saw her deep
green eyes go dark with passion. He kissed her
fiercely, possessively, while his hand claimed her
breasts again.

As he drank her in with his kiss, her fingers moved
deftly over his chest, unfastening his tie and buttons.
He reluctantly took his hands from her so he could
shrug out of his jacket and shirt. Then he eased her
back on the sofa and stretched out with her. He slid
his arms around her and continued where his trail
of kisses had left off. When his lips reached the top
of her breast, he felt his way to a rosy peak and
claimed it with his lips and tongue.

At the same time, he slid his fingers underneath
the lacy bit of elastic at her waist and pushed downward. After he'd freed himself and her of what re-

mained of their clothing, Clem moaned and arched her back to him, and he shifted his mouth from one breast to the other.

He felt his need for her in his loins, in his blood, his bones. It was a visceral need, spiraling out from the core of him like a vortex. His fingers slid down her hip and between her thighs, seeking her warmest, most feminine place, stroking, caressing. When her moans and movements told him the time was right, he positioned himself above her and eased himself downward.

She wrapped her arms around him and drew him closer until her face rested in the crook of his neck and shoulder. He thought he'd die when he felt her teeth nip at him. He entered her with maddening slowness, feeling her wriggle beneath him, urging him with her body to give more of himself and quickly, but he wouldn't be quick. He'd drive her as wild as she was driving him. He raised his head to look into her eyes, and he did see the wildness there, all the primitive, untamed passion—everything that had bewitched him from the first moment he saw her. It was all there in her forest-green eyes. He began to move, then, and she moved with him.

They were soaring, she thought—soaring to the sun, where they'd incinerate from the heat they made. The climax wracked her body, exploding a sphere of white light behind her eyes. In seconds she felt him shudder, and knew he was with her at the apex. Sparks rained down on them for a moment, it seemed. She tightened the muscles in her entire body, savoring the last of their oneness, already dreading their separation.

They held each other for several long moments before Clem opened her eyes to see Will looking down at her, his gaze full of tenderness. "Well," he said huskily, "I surely saw the stars. Did you?"

Clem reached up and took his face in her hands. "The whole galaxy."

Clem lit the candles in the elegant silver candle-holders and stood back to get the full effect. She'd set the dining table with the linen, china, and crystal she'd found in the sideboard, and if she did say so herself, the table was gorgeous. Maybe she could get the hang of sophisticated living, after all. She was going to try, anyway, try her best to fit into Will's world.

Will. She closed her eyes and hugged herself as she thought about the passionate weekend they'd just spent together. Their first time, on the roof, was just the beginning. He had awakened something in her that she never knew existed. She'd never felt so fulfilled as she did in his arms. That was why she had decided to give his proposal a chance.

Proposal. A shadow of uncertainty passed over Clem as she thought about what Will had said to her on the roof. *I want you to stay.* He hadn't asked her to marry him, just to stay with him—but then, they'd only known each other a couple of weeks, after all. It really wasn't unreasonable, she told herself, for two people to live together for a while before they married, to see if they could get along—especially when their backgrounds were as different as hers and Will's. No, not unreasonable at all.

She took off the apron she'd been wearing over her green silk dress and returned to the kitchen to check on dinner. Will had said he liked the dress because it brought out the green in her eyes. She wanted everything about tonight's dinner to be perfect. In fact, she'd spent all day planning, shopping, and cooking to make sure that it was. She might have set the table with fancy china and crystal, but Will was going to get a traditional southern meal. It seemed ages since she'd made her special cornbread, but it smelled wonderful.

Today was Monday, Will's first day back at work after his vacation. It had been so hard to say good-bye to him that morning, knowing their constant togetherness was at an end. At the same time, though, she had gotten the most delicious, satisfying feeling from kissing her man good-bye and sending him off to work.

She laughed out loud as she stirred the pot of Brunswick stew. Who'd have believed that Clem Harper would turn domestic practically overnight? Even more startling, who would have believed she would consider giving up her mountains to live in the city? But then, she'd never dreamed she would feel this way about a man.

Clem returned to the living room and surveyed the effects of her minor decorating touches. With just a vase of fresh flowers here, a colorful table runner there, she'd managed to liven up the cold apartment with her own, personal touch—at least a little, anyway. She sighed with satisfaction. Everything was perfect, and Will should be home any minute.

The telephone rang. When she heard Will's voice, her heart leapt a little, as if it had been weeks since she'd heard it instead of only a few hours.

"How was your day, sweetheart? Did you manage without me?" he asked in a teasing tone.

Clem closed her eyes and savored the rich timbre of his voice. "Just barely. But I did manage to put together a nice dinner for us. Will you be home soon?"

"Well, that's why I called you. I'm going to be late. Something important has come up, and I won't be there for quite a while. I hope dinner will keep. Is it something that I can heat up later?"

Clem sank down onto the cold white sofa. "Yes . . . sure. It'll be here when you get here. Do you have any idea when you'll be able to make it?"

"It's such a madhouse here you probably shouldn't expect me before eleven, but I can't be sure. These things seem to come up all the time, and you just never know how long it will take to work them out. So just hang in there, and I'll be there as soon as I can. I promise."

"Sure." Clem tried to keep the disappointment out of her voice.

"I can't wait to see you," he whispered.

"Hurry," she said, but she'd already heard the click that let her know he'd hung up.

She looked down and saw the reflection of an unhappy woman in the immaculate, chrome and glass coffee table. It was quite a shock, that face. Just a few minutes ago, she'd been practically walking on air, and now she looked as if she'd lost her best friend. Suddenly, her expression took on a look of determination and resolve. She sprang up from the sofa and walked briskly through the kitchen to the dining room. She would not let this setback upset her. Naturally he was swamped at work. He'd been on vacation for the last week. It was just one meal, for goodness sake, and there would be many, many romantic dinners for her and Will.

Clem took one last look at her handiwork—the

flowers, the table setting. Then she sighed, and blew out the candles.

The following Friday afternoon Clem stood in front of the apartment's floor-to-ceiling window, watching the rain run down the glass in rivulets. The downpour wasn't about to let up, and she felt so trapped in the apartment that she thought she would scream. Picking up her sketchpad, she flipped the pages over one by one. Bad. Worse. Pathetic. She threw the pad across the room and flung herself down on the white sofa, which seemed to get harder and more uninviting the more she sat on it. *I'd better enjoy that show tomorrow night, because it's probably the last one I'll ever have. Mine will be the shortest New York art career on record.*

The morning after Monday's ruined romantic dinner, she'd taken up her sketchpad to work out some designs, the way she'd done a thousand times before. Nothing came to her. She'd even taken her pad and pencils to Central Park, thinking that nature would inspire her, as it always had. Still nothing. There were just too many distractions—rollerbladers, baby carriages, picnics, Frisbee games. There were too many people around. Nature wasn't enough—she needed solitude. Then she'd seen a woman walking ten dogs at once, certainly a sight you didn't see every day in the Carolina mountains. One of the dogs, a golden retriever, reminded her of Ruby, and she burst into tears. She missed her dog. She missed her uncle. She missed her mountains.

* * *

Will was the only thing that had kept her from going insane. The days might have been hell, but the nights had been heaven. Clem felt a blush come to her cheeks as she remembered the week of lovemaking that had left her breathless, exhausted, and feeling more loved than she ever had in her life.

Clem glanced at her watch, a tacky souvenir one with a big apple in the center that Will had insisted on buying her. Five o'clock. She'd given up on expecting him home at a reasonable hour. Monday had not been an isolated incident—he'd been late every night this week. He'd promised to make it home by six last night, but he'd come in at eight instead, all apologetic and laden with cartons of Chinese food as a peace offering. As time went on, how much of Will's time would she get?

The phone rang. Since it was Friday night, it was probably Will calling to tell her what kind of restaurant they were going to, and when to be ready. She answered eagerly. "Hello?"

"Clem. Judith here. Listen, Will asked me to call you. He's tied up in a very important meeting, and won't be able to make it home for dinner. As a matter of fact, he'll probably be quite late, but he said he'd try to call you later."

"Oh. All right." Clem detected a note of sympathy in Judith's voice that was as unwelcome as it was insincere.

"Will's invited several of us to your show tomorrow night, so I'll see you then."

"Great. I'll see you at the gallery. Thanks for calling."

Clem put down the receiver and sank back onto the couch, wishing she could disappear into its cushions. So this was how it was going to be. Last week, when she'd had Will all to herself, had been a beautiful dream. This week was reality.

Shortly before midnight, Will opened the door to the apartment and was greeted by a sorrowful wail that made his blood go cold. He'd heard the sound before, and would never forget it. Clem was having another nightmare. He hurried to the bedroom, tossing aside his briefcase and jacket. From the light through the doorway, he could see her thrashing in her bedclothes.

He stood over her, wondering if he should wake her. From the way she fought, this nightmare must be even worse than the one she'd had their first night on the camping trip. A sheen of perspiration bathed her upper body, and she shuddered in a sudden chill.

He sat on the edge of the bed and gathered her into his arms, rocking her gently. She made a kitten-like whimpering sound that sank into his soul like a knife. He hadn't been able to banish her fears. He hadn't been able to make everything perfect.

Clem stirred in his arms. "I had a nightmare."

"A bad one?" Will helped her sit up and rubbed her shoulders.

"As bad as I used to have when I was a kid." She hung her head. "I hope these dreams aren't back to stay."

Will smoothed back her tousled hair. "You're probably just nervous about the show. You'll be more relaxed after it's over and things get back to normal."

Back to normal. Clem thought about the last week and shivered. A few hours of his time here and there would not be enough. Not here in the city. If they lived in the mountains, she could keep herself occupied with her own work and interests, but her creativity was dead here. She'd always thought of herself as an independent, self-sufficient woman—the polar opposite of needy, clinging vine types she used to feel sorry for—but here she found she needed Will more than she ever wanted to need anybody. That knowledge frightened her more than the fox in her dream. Seized by a sickening dread, she flung her arms around Will's neck.

"It's going to be all right," he said, stroking her back. "We're going to have a wonderful life together. You'll see. Why, we'll—"

Clem cut off his words with her kisses. She couldn't stand to hear any more. Squeezing her eyes shut to keep the tears from coming, she pulled him down onto the bed.

The next morning Clem wandered through Central Park, her emotions in turmoil. The show was that night, which was enough to put her nerves on edge, but that was the least of her problems. Afterward, Will would expect an answer to his invitation to live with him.

She'd thought the walk in the park might clear her head, but it hadn't. She felt almost as confined here as she had in the apartment, where she'd left Will talking business to associates on the phone. Even on a Saturday morning, he was still at work. Clem kicked a soda can out of her path and sat down on a park bench.

She leaned forward, propping her elbows on her knees, and hung her head. Staring down at the sidewalk, she saw a tiny, delicate flower growing out of a small crack in the large expanse of concrete. The tender purple petals looked alone and vulnerable in their concrete prison. Stuck there in the hard, unyielding fissure, the flower would eventually die, because it couldn't spread its roots, and could get no nourishment there even if it could.

Clem put her head in her hands and began to cry softly.

That night Clem peered out the window of the limo headed downtown, but didn't see a thing. "What if they don't like it? What if they don't like my stuff?"

"Not a chance," Will put his hand over hers to quiet their fidgeting. "You're going to be a huge success."

She wished she was as confident as Will. She took some comfort in the fact that she wasn't the only artist being showcased that night. There were a sculptor and a painter on the bill, as well. If worst came to worst, Clem thought, she could always let them take the spotlight and try to fade into the background.

When they arrived at the gallery, Elaine was the first one to greet them. "What a handsome couple you two make," she said, taking Clem's hands in her own. "Here, let's put some jewelry on you."

Clem was decked out for the occasion in a gown Mrs. Malcolm had selected for her—a twenties-inspired sleeveless, ankle-length sheath of turquoise. Elaine selected a necklace that featured a silver cat with lapis eyes. "There. That complements your gown perfectly. Now, you mustn't be nervous. You're going to be a sensation."

Clem tried to manage a smile. "Thanks for giving

me this opportunity. I can't tell you how much I appreciate it."

"It's my pleasure to work with an artist of your potential. Now let's take a look at your display." Elaine led Clem and Will to the display of Clem's work. The various pieces were attractively arranged on black velvet among chunks of raw crystals. The lighting showed each necklace, bracelet, and earring to its best advantage.

"Elaine, everything looks great. You've outdone yourself." Will put his arm around the older woman's shoulders.

Clem immediately felt better. Her work did look great, at that. "It's perfect."

"If the artist is happy, I'm happy." Elaine beamed. She was wearing her trademark black—a simple, floor-length gown with a high neck and long sleeves. She had chosen another of Clem's creations to wear—a butterfly with tourmaline-studded wings. "Now let me introduce you to the other artists."

Will and Clem chatted with the sculptor and the painter for a few minutes, and then Will excused himself, leaving her in the middle of a discussion of aesthetics. She nodded seriously whenever the sculptor, an earnest looking young man with old-fashioned spectacles and wild red hair, made a particularly impassioned point. The painter, a woman in a sixties retro granny dress of a floral print, punctuated the conversation with serious, well-thought-out questions whose meanings Clem could only guess.

Will returned in a few moments with champagne for Clem and himself, and they excused themselves to see the rest of the exhibit. "A glass of your favorite beverage to calm your nerves and fortify your spirit?"

"I thought you'd never ask." Clem took the glass

and sipped gratefully. "Now, those two really look like artists," she said, pointing at the sculptor and the painter, still engaged in ardent conversation. "They're so intense, so . . . artsy. I could never be like them."

Will laughed. "That's what makes you such a breath of fresh air. You're unpretentious, natural. And don't you ever turn artsy on me."

As more and more patrons arrived, Clem stood near her own exhibit, shaking hands, answering questions, and accepting praise. At one point she found herself surrounded by a small throng, all with complimentary things to say about her work. She responded as graciously as she could to each remark, all the while marvelling that she was actually the center of attention at a real, live New York art gallery show.

Even though there were many pairs of eyes on her while she was in the middle of one particular crowd of admirers, she suddenly felt the gaze of one person. She looked up to see Will, standing alone some distance away. He was smiling his warm, approving smile. Without a word, he raised his glass. As her gaze locked with his, all other sights and sounds faded into the background, and time stood still. In that moment the world was perfect, just like the world of the prince and princess in the music box. In that instant of absolute clarity Clem knew for the first time that she was a success. She was sure of something else, too, if she hadn't been sure already. She loved him.

He had given her so much. He'd revived her career, shared his home, shared his life, and given her the most wonderful time of her life. How could she leave him? Surely he would be able to find more time for her than he had this past week, Clem told herself

He was just catching up on a backlog of work, that was it. She'd talk to him about it later, and they'd work out a compromise. For her part, she'd try even harder to make things work. If she tried hard enough, her creativity had to come back. Didn't it?

The magic moment dissolved into reality as she watched Will become surrounded. Three couples, people he obviously knew, had moved toward him upon entering the gallery. The men shook hands with him, each in turn. The women . . . Clem drew in a deep breath. The women were dressed in the height of fashion. Tall and slender, any of them could have just stepped off the cover of *Town and Country*. One of them was Judith.

She had forgotten that Judith was coming. Just when she'd gotten relatively comfortable with the situation, the old knot of anxiety formed in her stomach. Will was leading the group of people toward her.

When he reached her side, he put his arm around her shoulders. "Everyone. I'd like you to meet Clementine Harper."

Will introduced his friends. The men, including Judith's date, worked for Will. The other women were their wives. These people radiated wealth and power, from the cut of their tailored clothing to their cultured, northeastern, old money accents. The women nodded as they were introduced, giving Clem a subtle head-to-toe once-over that left her feeling exposed and inadequate. The nice people who had surrounded her before had disappeared. Perhaps the newcomers intimidated them as much as they had Clem.

After the introductions, the men formed a circle around Will, launching into what sounded like serious business talk. Judith stepped forward, linked arms with Clem, and turned to face the other women. "This is the woman I've been telling you about."

Clem swallowed hard. *Uh-oh.*

The women examined the display of Clem's work, murmuring half-hearted words of approval. "Interesting," Deirdre said. "You must be very proud," said Elizabeth.

Judith was making some complimentary remarks of her own when the other two women, obviously bored with the situation, began to make plans for some kind of girl's night out the following week.

"I couldn't possibly do it on Thursday," Deirdre insisted. "That's when Scott and I have our private time that we schedule for every other week."

Every other week? Clem tried to hide her alarm as she nodded absently, pretending to listen to Judith drone on about her knowledge of modern art.

Elizabeth gave her friend a jealous look. "Your husband gives you a whole night every other week, does he? I wish I could get Brandon to commit to that."

Judith was obviously listening to the other women's conversation, as well, for she chose that point to chime in. "Deirdre, of course you're free on Thursday. Didn't Scott tell you? He's going out of town on a business trip. We all are—Scott, Brandon, me, Will."

Clem could have sworn she felt an Arctic blast blow into the room. Deirdre and Elizabeth glared at Judith. Their husbands had obviously forgotten to tell them about the trip, as Will, Clem noted dismally, had forgotten to tell *her.* She waited for the women to tell Judith off, but instead they composed their expressions into doll-like blandness. "No, he didn't tell me. But thank you, Judith, as always, for setting things straight."

As much as the women had intimidated her, Clem actually felt a kinship with them now. Good old Judith had struck again. And, in their positions, there wasn't a damn thing they could say to her.

Judith smiled happily as the other two women turned away and strolled toward another exhibit. "Poor dears," Judith purred. "You'd think they'd be used to that sort of thing by now." She gave Clem a meaningful look. "It would be extremely difficult to be married to a man like Scott, or Brandon, or . . . Will. They're married to their careers, really. Their work is what they thrive on, what makes them who they are. I should know. I'm at their sides—ten, twelve, fourteen hours a day."

Clem felt as if she'd had the wind knocked out of her, and struggled to keep her composure. She knew she had to get away from this woman or she'd suffocate. "Excuse me, won't you? I see someone over there that I must say hello to."

Clem walked toward the back of the gallery, hoping to find a way out. She saw a lighted Exit sign at the end of the hallway that led to Elaine's office and made a dash for it. Once outside, she gasped, gulping in lungsful of air like a diver coming up from the depths of the ocean.

She stumbled out into the tiny courtyard and sat on a marble bench. She'd been a fool to think she could reach a compromise with Will over the hours he spent at work. Judith was right. He thrived on his work, just as Clem thrived on hers. She laughed bitterly. Judith just couldn't resist pointing out that even if Clem did wind up with Will, Judith would be the one by his side for most of his waking hours.

If only her creativity hadn't left her, perhaps she could learn to live with seeing Will a stolen hour here and there. But her ability to create was gone, and she no longer had her work to sustain her, not here where Will was. That meant she would be left with nothing.

And for what? Those women she'd met earlier were *wives*. At least they had commitment from their men, as empty as that commitment seemed. She wouldn't even have that if Will only asked her to live with him tonight.

The door opened and Elaine leaned out. "Clem. Just the person I was coming to find. Step in here for a moment, won't you?"

Clem reluctantly followed Elaine into the office. The desk was littered with slips of paper.

"You've done splendidly tonight, dear." Elaine made a sweeping gesture toward the pile of paper on her desk. On second glance, Clem could see mostly checks and charge slips. Elaine picked up one of the checks and held it out to her. "I haven't made the final accounting yet, but I want you to have this as a first installment."

Clem took the check and looked at it in disbelief. "Are you sure you didn't put too many zeros on here by mistake?"

Elaine laughed heartily. "I'm absolutely sure. But that check isn't the best part." Elaine took Clem's hand and led her to the loveseat. "You're going to have to sit down for this. I don't want you to faint." Elaine sat and pulled Clem down next to her.

"Do you remember that soft-spoken man with the goatee who asked you so many questions about how you come up with your designs, and the techniques you use?"

Clem nodded. The man had seemed keenly interested in her work, more than any of the other patrons she'd talked to tonight.

Elaine's eyes glowed. "Well, he's a buyer for a national chain of boutiques. And he wants to carry your jewelry in all of them. They'll even take care of the manufacturing. All you have to do is negotiate the contract to sell him the designs."

Clem could hardly believe her ears. "You're not kidding, are you?"

"No, dear." Elaine squeezed her hand as if to assure Clem that she wasn't dreaming.

"But I don't know how to negotiate a contract."

The older woman laughed. "It's easy. I've done it hundreds of times."

Clem looked at her hopefully. "Would you be my agent?"

"Of course, if that's what you want."

"It is." Clem breathed a sigh of relief.

The door opened and Will stuck his head through. "I wondered where you two disappeared to." Elaine motioned him in and indicated the chair opposite the loveseat. Clem let Elaine fill Will in on the results of the showing, including the offer from the boutique buyer, grateful for the time to try to regain her wits. Will was thrilled by the news of the sales, and also that Elaine was acting as Clem's agent.

Elaine and Will talked excitedly about the details of Clem's contract with the buyer—options for future designs and so on. Clem barely heard them. Future designs, they'd said. What future designs? There weren't going to be any as long as she stayed here. At least her financial worries were finally over for a while. She could go back home in triumph and live her life the way she'd always wanted.

She looked at Will as he and Elaine talked and

laughed. Would she have the strength to leave him if all he offered her was a living arrangement, and not a wedding ring?

As they walked back into the gallery, it was nearly closing time, and there were only a few people left. Will filled three glasses from the last bottle of champagne. He handed the women their glasses and then raised his own.

"I'd like to propose a toast," he said grandly. "Here's to long and fulfilling partnerships."

Clem clinked her glass against Elaine's and returned the older woman's smile. Then she turned to touch glasses with Will, and saw his meaningful look. Partnerships, he'd said. Plural. He hadn't been talking just about her arrangement with Elaine, but about her arrangement with him, as well. He was expecting an answer. Tonight. What would the question be?

Clem gulped her champagne. The bubbly liquid blazed a fiery trail down her throat. What was she going to do?

TWELVE

"You're awfully quiet for someone who just hit the jackpot, artistically speaking." Will put his arm around her and drew her close to him after they had settled into the limo for the return trip. "Wouldn't you like to go somewhere exciting and dance the night away to celebrate your success?"

Clem looked into his face, and the happiness she saw there nearly wrenched her heart from her body. "I'm too tired. Would you mind if we just went home?"

"Of course not," he said, bringing her head to his shoulder. "We've got all the time in the world to celebrate."

Clem caught her lower lip between her teeth. She looked away so that he could not see her face.

"That reminds me. Tonight was the night you were going to give me the answer to a very important question I asked you last week."

She took a deep breath. "And what question was that, exactly?"

He took her chin in his hand and turned her face to his. "Will you stay with me here in New York, Clem? Will you live with me?"

Clem blinked her eyes as his words sank in. He

didn't want to marry her. It didn't come as a surprise, really. Not after she'd seen the wives of his friends. She wasn't one of them, and never would be. Will just wanted a live-in girlfriend to warm his bed, not a wife the likes of her. Well, she wouldn't sacrifice everything just for that small role in his life. She'd leave, but before she did she'd make sure of one thing—he would never forget her.

She twisted her body toward him, wrapped her arms around his neck and covered his mouth with her own. She moved her leg up and over his, and a groan escaped his lips. He cupped her bottom with one hand as the other sought the zipper of her dress. "I'll take that as a yes," he said hoarsely as her hand slid down his chest, and lower still.

In the hour before dawn on Monday morning, Clem sat up in bed, leaning against the headboard while she watched Will sleep. She leaned forward on her arms, which were propped on her drawn up knees, naked except for the cotton sheet that covered her to her waist. Lightly, she brushed a lock of raven hair away from his forehead and let her fingers slide down his stubbly, unshaven cheek.

She closed her eyes, remembering the deliciously rough feel of his cheeks and chin on her breasts, her belly, her thighs. She shivered and pulled the sheet higher. Heat flooded her body when she thought about the reason why he had forgotten to shave yesterday—they had spent the whole day in bed. When she'd finally acknowledged that she was leaving him, a wildness had come over her that was difficult to explain. Perhaps she wanted to brand the feel of his body into her mind so she would always have him in her memory. Or maybe she was trying to get her fill of him once and for all, to satiate herself completely to lessen the pain of their separation, as if that were possible. Her passion had been instinctive, like that of an animal. The only shame she felt was that she hadn't had the guts to tell him she was leaving.

She'd tried to hate him for not wanting her as his wife, but she just couldn't do it. He couldn't help the way he was any more than she could help being a naive country girl. Besides, after all he had done for her, how could she not love him still?

Sitting there in the near darkness, she had decided what she would do. Tomorrow when he came home from work, she would be gone. She rationalized her decision by telling herself that if she told him face-to-face she was leaving, he wouldn't let her go—he would physically try to stop her—but deep down, she knew the truth. She was taking the coward's way out—something she had never done before. She would do it now, because it would spare her from having to look into those dusky blue eyes and tell him she was leaving. He would be just as hurt when he discovered she was gone, but she wouldn't have to be there to see it.

She went over everything in her mind for the hundredth time. There was no way out. She'd begun to realize it days ago, when she found her creativity had dried up and Will's job had intruded on her fantasy world. Then she'd met Will's friends and run headlong into even more harsh realities. She'd never fit in with the kind of people he knew, and the truth was, she didn't really want to. She loved Elaine, of course, but the wives of Will's peers had given her the creeps. Then there was Judith.

If she only had her work to fill up the lonely hours

without Will, but there would be no art, no creativity here. She would be a kept woman, in a gilded cage like the bird in the mythic story. Kept by a man she loved and who loved her, but dying inside just the same.

She longed to cry until she couldn't cry anymore, but she would save that for tomorrow. In the last twilight hour she had with him, she would love him, savor him, memorize every inch of his body. She stretched out beside him and rested her head on his shoulder. She laid her hand lightly on his chest, swirling her fingertips through the crisp, springy hair there. Leaning over him, she kissed his eyelids, his throat, the little jagged scar on his bicep. He stirred, and a smile passed over his face—a smile so sweet that Clem found she could not hold back all her tears, after all. A single teardrop fell, striking his chest right above his heart, like a dagger finding its deadly mark. Clem bore it away with her tongue before the sensation could wake him, but it was too late. His powerful arms came around her, pressing her tightly to him, as if they would never let her go. After a while she raised herself above his body and sought him, joining them together for the last time.

She'd been able to keep her composure until Will left for work. After she kissed him good-bye and closed the door behind him, she sank to the floor and cried. Then she picked herself up, showered, packed her things in her old duffle, and composed the letter she would leave on her bed. She couldn't bear to take the things he'd bought her, so she left them behind, all save the music box with its happy, perfect prince and princess. She couldn't imagine why she felt like taking the thing that made her the saddest, but she took it, anyway.

There was a branch of Elaine's bank within walking distance, so Clem was able to cash her check. That would allow her to fly home instead of taking the bus. She had no idea when the next flight to North Carolina was, but she'd wait at the airport as long as she had to, and take the first thing that was available. She would send Elaine her address and phone number as soon as she got back home.

With a last long look at Will's apartment building, Clem slung her bag over her shoulder and walked to the curb to hail a cab.

Clem boarded the plane a half hour later, stowed the duffle under the seat in front of her, and tried to get comfortable in her seat next to the window. There was much commotion and slamming of overhead bins as people settled themselves and their luggage into the cabin.

In a few minutes, a flight attendant came to stand in front of the bulkhead and asked for everyone's attention. She evidently wasn't getting through to this crowd, Clem noted, looking around her at the people thoroughly ignoring the woman. *How rude,* Clem thought. This nice lady clearly had something important to say.

A recording played a spiel of safety precautions as the attendant demonstrated the proper usage of a seatbelt and oxygen mask. Clem didn't know if she should be alarmed or comforted by the news that her seat cushion could be used as a flotation device.

What did it matter? Clem leaned back and closed her eyes. The trip through the maze of the air termi-

nal and the anticipation of her first plane ride all had
distracted her for a while, but now all she could think
about was Will—and the fact that in a few hours he
would find that awful, hateful, cowardly letter. He
would be hurt—for a while, anyway. Then he would
find someone else. Probably someone like those
women she'd met at her show.

Soon the plane began to taxi toward the runway,
a strange sensation that Clem found she rather liked.
The plane took a ninety degree turn and became still
for a few seconds. Its mighty engines began to roar
and Clem felt a surge of power from all around her.
Then the great bird began to move. Faster and faster
it strained forward, until Clem thought the force of
its speed would break it apart. There was a release,
and suddenly Clem was a creature of the air and not
of the earth. She squeezed her eyes shut and savored
the sensation of flight. She was free. Free! Out of the
gilded cage and soaring toward the sun.

"Can't you go any faster, buddy?" Will never
thought he would hear himself say those words to a
New York City cab driver. The cabbie grinned and
gave him the thumbs-up sign as he stamped the ac-
celerator hard enough to force Will back into the
seat. Will laughed out loud at himself. It was true
what people said—that love makes you do funny
things—and he was a love-sodden fool if ever there
was one.

Who could blame him? The past weekend had
been the most incredible of his life. From the time
Clem had wrapped her arms—and legs—around him
in the limo until right before he had to shower for
work this morning, she had behaved as if she couldn't

get enough of him. He had asked her for her decision about living with him. Rather than telling him, in typical Clementine fashion, she'd chosen to show him—and he'd thought *last* week had been exciting.

Winning Clem's heart had been the challenge he'd been looking for, and he'd finally succeeded. Looking back over the events of the last two weeks, he mentally congratulated himself on the way he'd handled her. Sure, there were rough moments—that time with the hansom cab horse, and the return of her nightmares—but they were only temporary setbacks. He'd finally tamed the wild child, and it had been a helluva lot more fun than a leveraged buyout. Now she was his—the sweetest prize he'd ever won.

He bounded from the cab after paying the driver, delighted to see a pushcart full of flowers right in front of his building. Luck was with him, no doubt about it. He bought two dozen red roses from the vendor and gave Mike the doorman a hearty slap on the back on his way through the entrance.

"Honey, I'm home!" Geez, he never thought he'd hear himself say *that,* either. Clem wasn't in the kitchen or the living room. That could only mean one thing—she was lying in wait for him in the bedroom. He put the flowers down on an end table and started down the hallway. "Baby, you're going to be the death of me!" She wasn't there, either.

"Clem!" By the time he reached her old bedroom, he was anxious. He flung the door open and saw that she wasn't there, either. He strode across the room, thinking that perhaps she was taking a soak in the tub. He relaxed a little when he passed by the open closet and noticed that the outfits he'd bought her were still hanging there. She wasn't in the bathroom.

It was then that he saw the piece of paper on the

bed, a page out of Clem's sketchbook. Instead of the bold lines of one of her sketches, it was covered with her neat, small script. It was a note. Icy fingers of dread clutched at Will's stomach as he stared at it. He tried to shake off the feeling, but it wouldn't budge. If Clem had simply gone for takeout food or was on some other errand, a few scrawled words of explanation would suffice. But there were many words on this paper. It was not so much a note as a letter. He walked toward it slowly. The hand that reached for the letter seemed disembodied from him, and shook slightly as he picked it up.

His gaze skimmed across the words, registering key phrases: *thank you . . . most wonderful time . . . sorry . . . feel like a coward . . . can't create any more . . . feel trapped . . . no time together . . . demands of your job . . . no choice . . . please forgive . . . love you forever . . .*

She was gone. He couldn't understand it. He'd done all the right things, laid all the right groundwork. When you do all that, everything should fall into place, just like with stock issues, mergers, takeovers. Only Clem wasn't any of those things. She was a woman. The only one he'd ever loved. His strength suddenly left him, and he sank to his knees. As one hand clutched the letter, the other came to rest on the floor, where it touched something silky.

Her black slip lay crumpled on the carpet. His mind went into a flashback so vivid it was almost a hallucination. A flashback to the last time he'd seen that slip in a crumpled heap on the floor, the night Clem had first given herself to him, the first night he'd been fool enough to think that she was his. He dropped the letter and lifted the filmy wisp of cloth with both hands. As the scent of her perfume drifted up to him, he buried his face in the material and heard himself bellow in pain.

He didn't know how long he knelt there, or what finally made him get up again. He tossed the slip and the letter on the bed and turned to go. Then he saw Clem's collection of the knickknacks he had bought her—the miniature Empire State Building, the I Love New York magnet, and the rest of the trinkets—all lined up neatly on her dresser. He picked up a snow globe and shook it. Hundreds of particles of plastic snow swirled around a *New York Is for Lovers* sign. He drew back and dashed the glass ornament against the wall, shattering it into a thousand pieces.

He looked into the dresser's mirror, hardly recognizing himself as this pale man with bloodshot eyes and tousled hair. "Fool!" he said to the strange reflection. "You never needed a new challenge. You needed Clem, and you still do. Now think of a way to get her back."

Clem hauled her duffle out of the back of her friend Mark's pickup truck and returned to the passenger window to say good-bye. "Thanks for the ride. I owe you one."

"Don't mention it. Say hello to Jess for me." With that, Mark was on his way and Clem turned to look at Uncle Jess's cabin. She had come straight here to get Ruby and to talk to Uncle Jess, her closest confidante for as far back as she could remember. If ever she needed some reassuring words, it was now, although she didn't think there was anything anyone could ever say to make her feel any better.

The door to the cabin was open and Clem could see Jess in his chair, asleep, his arms crossed over his massive belly. The sight comforted her more than any soothing words could have done. She had to smile in spite of her somber mood as she stepped onto the bottom step of the cabin's front porch. A fuzzy face peeked around the door frame, its ears springing to attention. In an instant, the rest of the dog followed, bounding down the steps and hitting Clem squarely in the stomach.

"Well, hello to you, too," Clem said after her breath returned. She hugged the ecstatic Ruby, who licked her face generously.

By that time, Jess had made his way to the doorway and accepted a kiss on the cheek as she came into the room. "So, how'd it go? Did you knock 'em dead?"

Clem winced at Jess's choice of words as she tossed the duffle in a corner. Will would be on the receiving end of her stab-in-the-back Dear John letter right about now. "You could say that."

She sprawled out in her favorite cushy chair and told Jess all about the things she'd seen in New York—from the skyscrapers and Broadway plays to the fancy food and champagne. She had related some of this to him on the phone from New York, of course, but she'd saved some of the best parts to tell him in person because she wanted to see his face.

Jess grinned and slapped his knee. "How're we going to keep you down in the shop after you've seen New York?" he teased.

"Don't you worry about that. I'm here to stay, and I'm going to work in our shop and set my own hours, just like I always have."

Having saved the news about the show until last, Clem delighted in seeing the expression on the old man's face when she told him how much money she had made already, and when she told him about the contract with the boutique buyer, she was rewarded with a whoop of joy.

"I knew you could do it, gal! That'll keep us in business until judgment day. Our worries are over."

Clem managed a smile, but it was forced and Jess knew it. Of course she'd phoned Jess when she decided to stay in New York with Will those two weeks. He must have been wondering how the relationship turned out.

The old man scratched his chin and his eyebrows drew together. "How'd you leave things with old what's-his-name?"

Clem sighed and said simply, "It's over." Jess knew her well enough to leave it at that.

"I'm sorry. I guess some things have a way of working out for the best."

Clem realized for the first time that she was exhausted—mentally and physically. She said good-bye to Jess, took up her duffle, and headed for her own cabin, Ruby at her heels.

She let the serenity of the forest surround her, from the azure sky overhead to the spongy earth beneath her feet. The wind stirred her hair as an elder would fondly tousle the hair of a favorite child. The swaying of the pine boughs overhead brought a gentle whisper, ancient and primitive, to Clem's ears. Although the pain remained, her soul was flooded with peace. She was home.

Clem sat on the bank of the pond near her house, with her fishing pole staked down on one side of her and Ruby napping on the other. On her lap was her sketchpad. It was taking all Clem's restraint not to throw the cursed thing into the water. After two weeks of being back home, she still hadn't come up with anything worth a damn. On top of that, the fish weren't biting. She leaned back against the pine tree she was sitting under and closed her eyes. She'd been sure that her creativity would return once she came home, but something still wasn't right. It was Will. She missed him so desperately that she could hardly think of anything else.

She felt Ruby stir beside her and give a little whine. Probably another one of her doggie dreams. Clem hadn't been sleeping so well herself, lately.

She'd followed her heart when she'd thought that it was leading her back home to the mountains, but she was still not happy. Part of her heart was back in New York with Will—it was broken in two.

A hawk flew overhead, and Clem looked up at it. She had to figure out how to get her heart back together again. Maybe then her creativity would return. How could she do that? She couldn't be in two places at one time.

Clem scrambled to her feet as her fishing pole was jerked out of the forked stick on which it was anchored and plunged toward the pond. She grabbed it right before it submerged completely, and reeled in a fine, fat fish. Ruby roused and thumped her tail against the pine straw.

As Clem put the fish on the stringer, she thought about the story of the caged bird who got to keep her freedom and her brave warrior. Maybe she *could* be in both places, just not at the same time.

Clem was baiting her hook again when she started violently at the sound of a chainsaw cranking up nearby. Nobody should be cutting firewood in that part of the forest. The nearest house was a half mile

away, and that was the unoccupied Mitchell place—
which was now Will's place.

Clem put down her fishing pole. She was techni-
cally on Will's land, and the troubling whine of the
saw was coming from Will's property, as well. What
did it mean? She started off in the direction of the
sound with a sinking feeling in her heart. Slapping
vines and brambles out of her way without regard to
the briars raking her skin, she ran through the trees
and undergrowth for several minutes until she
reached a little glade up the mountain from the
Mitchell place. It was one of her favorite places in
the forest, one of the places she'd camped when she
was on the run as a teenager. Now it was crowded
with men wielding chainsaws and crosscut saws. If this
were not disturbing enough, to Clem's horror one
of the men revved up a small earth moving machine
and began pushing over small pines.

She leaned against a tree and tried to catch her
breath. She felt as if someone had knocked the wind
out of her. Her breathlessness was not from her mad
dash through the woods. Will had sold the land—just
as he'd said he would. He had sold to developers,
and they were about to cut down all the trees and
put up goodness knew what. Ruby, who'd followed
her through the forest, whined pitifully as another
saw started up, her sensitive ears laid back in a clear
indication of her disapproval.

When she'd gotten her breath back and pulled
herself together, Clem approached the man who
seemed to be in charge, the one who was giving orders to the others. She had to know what was going
on.

"Excuse me," Clem began when she'd caught up
to him. The man turned toward her without the least

indication of surprise at being approached by a woman in the middle of the forest. "I was fishing in a stream over the ridge," Clem continued, waving her hand vaguely in the direction from which she had come, "and I heard the saws. I live near here and I was wondering—I mean, you're obviously clearing this land. Could you tell me what's going to be built here—and who's building it?"

"Sorry, ma'am, but I'm not at liberty to tell you that. Begging your pardon, but I'm going to have to ask you to leave the area. We don't want to injure anybody while we're cutting trees. Insurance. You understand."

Clem nodded and moved away down the hillside. She whistled for Ruby to follow her and made her way toward Will's cabin. She had to know what was going to happen to her world. Had Will sold the land to developers who would put up a resort? A strip shopping center? A discount store? If they were going to build something harmless, like a few private homes, then why wouldn't they just tell her? Why the secrecy?

When she reached sight of the cabin, she saw that the workmen had parked their trucks in the driveway. She peeked into one of the cabin's widows and determined that there was nobody there. Then she crept from pickup truck to pickup truck, looking in the cab of each. In the third truck, she saw a clipboard lying on the bench-style seat. The paper on top of the board looked like a fax of some kind. With a glance over each shoulder, Clem opened the pickup door and reached inside for the clipboard. The paper was a work order for landscaping a tract of land. The work order was signed by Will Fletcher. Clem squeezed her eyes shut. It wasn't some anonymous developer who was despoiling her beloved mountains. It *was* Will.

She replaced the clipboard and closed the truck door as quietly as she could. She couldn't believe it. Had Will been planning to develop this land the whole time she'd known him, or was he just doing it now to spite her—to pay her back for the cruel way that she had left him? Was she the cause of this? She couldn't bear the idea.

What had she done?

THIRTEEN

A week later, Clem tossed the morning mail onto her workbench and sat down. The sight of the bills didn't disturb her as much now, since she could actually pay them—for a while, anyway. The sketches for the new line were abysmal. The boutique buyer wouldn't be amused when it was time for Clem to present them.

On the bottom of the stack, she saw a large envelope bearing the logo of Elaine's gallery. She hastily tore it open to find the promised contract from the boutique buyer. When she came to the proffered dollar figure, she stared at it for a moment, savoring it. She'd known what to expect, of course, having discussed it with Elaine several times on the phone, but there was something fine about seeing the sum in black-and-white.

The satisfaction she felt in being able to shore up her business could not compensate for her lingering sense of loss, however. In their conversations Elaine had never once mentioned Will, and neither had Clem, of course. She hadn't heard from him directly, either, which wasn't surprising, since she'd asked him in her letter not to contact her. She didn't know what was worse, the pain of losing Will or his apparent willingness to let her go.

If he would still have her, maybe she could divide her time between New York and the mountains. First she had to work up the nerve to call him. She wanted to talk to him about their relationship, about the development he had planned, about so many things, but the wonderful sense of security she'd once felt with Will was gone. Now she had nothing but fear where he was concerned.

She feared that by this time he had found another woman to occupy his heart—and his bed. She remembered the doll-like, shallow women she'd met at the show, and shivered. Her biggest fear—the one that kept her awake nights—was that he hated her for the cowardly way in which she had left him. After what they'd meant to each other, what she'd done might be unforgivable. She wouldn't blame him if he never wanted to speak to her again.

Then there was the newest fear—the one about her perfect little world being turned an eyesore infested by neon and asphalt—by none other than Will Fletcher. It had crossed her mind that he might be doing all this for spite—it was certainly within his power—but she knew Will too well for that. Despite his toughness in the business world, he didn't have a hateful bone in his body. It was his inherent goodness and generosity that she loved most about him. That was before she'd hurt him, though.

Her hand hovered above the telephone and then dropped to her side. She'd call him as soon as she figured out what she would say. She could beg him not to go forward with the development, but she had no right—not after the way she'd behaved.

She stashed the mail in the drawer of her workbench and took up her sketchpad and pencil, vaguely aware of the crunch of tires on the gravel outside. It was the height of the tourist season, and her customer traffic had picked up the last few days. She heard footsteps coming up the stairs of the shop.

"Be with you in a minute," she called as she added a few more strokes to another in a long line of sketches she didn't like very much.

"Take your time," came a rumbling, masculine voice. "I'm just looking."

Clem would have recognized that deep, rich voice if she'd lived to be two hundred. And he *was* looking. She could feel his stare nearly boring a hole through her, and she wasn't even looking back. She froze, not daring to look up, not knowing what she would do if she did. Would she run? Would she throw herself into his arms? Finally, with agonizing slowness, she forced her gaze upward and into the ice blue gaze of the man she loved.

His face was impassive, impossible to read. He hated her. She knew it. He'd probably come to check up on the building project and just stopped off to give her a piece of his mind. She didn't blame him.

"How've you been?" she heard herself say stupidly.

"Lousy. And you?"

"The same."

Will braced his broad hands on top of the counter, as if for support, or perhaps restraint. He probably wanted to throttle her. He wore one of his immaculate business suits. Here was Will the businessman, not Will the outdoorsman. He was definitely not on vacation this time.

"Listen," she began. "About the way I left—"

Will held up his hand. "You tried. I know that."

"I did," she said quickly. "But I just couldn't stay.

And I didn't have the guts to tell you to your face. You understand that, don't you?"

"Of course."

Clem guessed she should be glad Will didn't seem to want to strangle her, but his understanding made her feel even more wretched than she had when she thought he was angry.

"So what brings you back?" Drawn to him, she stood up and walked in his direction. The counter stood between them as a physical barrier. She leaned against it to steady her shaking legs.

"A business venture."

He stared at her, letting his gaze boldly roam the length of her body. She nervously smoothed the skirt of her simple cotton dress and looked down to keep from having to meet his eyes. "I've seen," she said quietly.

"The building site, you mean."

"Yes."

"I didn't figure it would escape your notice."

Clem lifted her chin and looked at him evenly. "Some location."

Returning her level gaze impassively, he said, "I know it's one of your favorite spots."

Clem took a deep breath. If his casual attitude toward ruining one of her favorite spots on earth was meant to hurt her, it was succeeding. "So, what are you building?"

"We'll talk about that another time. Now, about that letter—"

"Will, please don't," Clem begged. As unpleasant as the subject of the building project was, her feelings about her split with him were still raw and painful.

She started to take a step away from him. She wasn't quick enough, and he reached over the counter, seizing her by the upper arms. He walked her to the end of the counter, and pulled her through the little swinging door which led to the area that housed her workbench. She was on his side of the counter now, and he was pressing her against it, forcing her to look at him.

"We're going to talk about this. You owe me that much," he said, his blue eyes brooking no opposition. "Tell me. Is it me?" he asked, holding her gaze fixed with his own. "Am I the reason you were unhappy? Am I the reason you feel your creativity has gone? Did I . . . stifle you?"

Clem brought her hand to his cheek. "No. You were wonderful. It wasn't you. It was just that I wasn't where I feel like I belong. I wasn't here in the mountains anymore.

"It was great when we were together all the time. Then you started back to work, and I only got to see you for a couple of hours a day. I started to feel like that caged bird in the story. I had to fly. I had to be free."

A flash of pain played across his features. "I neglected you. I know that now. And believe me, I'm sorry. It's just that I had so many people who were depending on me."

Clem put her fingers gently on his lips. "I understand. I really do. But you have to understand that for me to move to the city—I just needed more of you. And besides, after I saw you with your friends at the gallery, I knew I could never fit in with them. They're sophisticated, worldly, educated, cultured—"

"Clem," he interrupted, not loosening his grip on her arms. "I didn't want you to be like them. I fell in love with you because you're different, fresh, exciting—"

"I may be exciting to you now, but how long before the new wears off of me, and all that's left is a country girl who doesn't fascinate you anymore?"

He shook his head vehemently. "It's not like that. Your appeal is so much more for me. You don't realize how special you are." He gathered her hands into his. "I'm sure my feelings for you are real."

"Will, please. This can't work out. We can't live in each other's worlds."

He stared at her for a long moment. What was he thinking? she wondered. Had the truth of her words sunk in at last? An expression of resignation came over his face, but it had an intensity that told her the debate was not necessarily over as far as he was concerned.

He relaxed somewhat. "All right. I just want to know one more thing."

"What?" she said breathlessly.

She looked into his eyes and saw the coldness melt into anguish. "Did you mean it? What you said in your letter?"

Clem nodded. "Yes. All of it."

"I'm talking about the last part. Just the last part."

Clem tried to think. What had she said last? They were so close she could feel his breath on her face, and it was coming as hard and as fast as her own. Then she remembered. Her very last words were that she loved him. *Forever.*

"Yes," she said. "I do mean it."

His arms went around her in a ferocious hug and his lips covered hers. She melted against him, clutching at this man she'd thought she'd never touch again. After a moment, he released her lips and held her as she sagged against him, her head coming to rest on his shoulder.

"Now, about that business venture," he said calmly.

Clem looked up at him and blinked, unable to believe his rapid shift from a passionate kiss to matter-of-fact business talk. "What?"

He took her arms and set her away from him. His eyes unreadable once again, he said, "Meet me at the building site at two o'clock."

Clem steadied herself. "All right." This was it. He had come to make sure that she still loved him before they parted for good. Then he'd show her the courtesy of letting her in on his plans, and he'd leave because he thought that's what she wanted. She *didn't* want him to leave, but what she wanted couldn't be. How could she have both Will and her beloved mountains?

Will nodded and turned to go. Numbly, she followed him out of the shop and down the steps. Once they'd reached the ground he turned to her again, put his arms around her, more gently this time, and kissed her tenderly. He pressed her against him, and his hands moved over her from her neck to her shoulders, waist, and hips, as if he were trying to memorize her every curve. It was, she realized brokenheartedly, a good-bye kiss.

He let her go again and strode to his car, stopping only to give Ruby an affectionate pat on the head. He drove away, not once looking back.

Clem sank onto the steps. At least she would see him one more time. At two o'clock.

At two sharp, Clem stepped into the clearing. The little glen that she'd loved so as a child had a gaping hole in it where earthmoving machinery had scooped out a space for a large building. Small stakes with

colored flags indicated the dimensions of the thing.
Whatever it was, it was huge. Most of the lovely flow-
ering bushes remained, for now. There would be a
big parking lot, of course, and the flowers would be
no more.

In the middle of the clearing stood Will, intently
staring at a set of blueprints he'd unrolled. He was
so enthralled by the building plans that he didn't see
her at first. When he did, he rolled up the plans and
gestured for her to follow him. She followed him
around the hole in the ground and up the hill to the
place right above, where the machines had hollowed
the space out of the hillside.

When he reached the summit, he held out his
hand for her. "Be careful," he cautioned. "Don't fall.
It's steep up here."

She took his hand and stood beside him, the skirt
of her cotton dress blowing slightly in the breeze.
Together they looked out over the valley below, the
gentle hues of the evergreens giving way here and
there to the brighter colors of summer vegetation in
full bloom. The valley was dotted by the homesteads
of families who'd lived there for generations. Their
vegetable gardens were laid out in neat rows, their
flower gardens ablaze in more riotous patches of
color.

Her eyes clouded with tears. This was the best view
in the county, the view she'd loved all her life. She
supposed he'd led her here to enjoy it one more
time, before the building he was putting up ob-
structed it completely. She supposed she should
thank him for that, at least. She closed her eyes, trying to remember this breathtaking sight. She felt
Will's arms go around her tightly.

"Keep your eyes closed, Clem," he whispered, his

lips brushing her eyelids and brow. "You're a story-teller, the best I've ever heard. Think about us. How is our story going to end? Tell us a happy ending, Clem. Can you do that?"

"Wha—what do you mean?"

Will's breath was warm against her cheek. "If your life could be any way you wanted . . . how would it be?"

She opened her eyes and looked at him. "If I could have anything I wanted, I would have you . . . right here, forever." Clem felt her body quake, and she started to tremble.

It was Will's turn to close his eyes. He looked as if he was savoring what she'd just said. After a moment, he took a deep breath and began to speak. "This is where our bedroom will be," he said in a reverent tone, his voice breaking slightly. "This is where we will conceive our children."

Clem's eyes widened. "What? What do you mean?"

Will unleashed a smile that melted her heart. "This is our house, Clem. That is, if you'll have me."

"But how?" Clem couldn't have heard what she thought she had. Was her admittedly legendary imagination running away with her?

Will placed his hand on her forehead and smoothed back the hair that the breeze had swirled around her face. "The business venture I mentioned to you earlier was not about the building. It was about my new career. Now that I'm sure of your feelings for me, I can finalize my plans. I'm going to resign from the investment firm and start publishing my own financial newsletter. It's the challenge I've been looking for, and I can do it from right here."

Clem stared blankly, uncomprehending.

He reached up to stroke her cheek. "You see, when

I first came here, I was unhappy. I was burned out, dissatisfied. I thought I needed a new challenge. Then I met you, and I thought you were that challenge. I was going to tame the wild child, bring her to New York, and make her mine." He took a deep breath and let his lips brush her forehead before continuing. "What I didn't understand then, but do now, is that you're not a challenge to be conquered. You're a woman to be loved for who she is.

"When you left, I nearly fell apart. I started to re-evaluate my goals and priorities, and decided that I'd do whatever it took to be with you. And if that meant leaving Manhattan and joining you here in the mountains, at least part-time, that's what I would do. I know you tried, really tried, to make things work with me in New York. But you had to come back here because, as you said, it's where you belong. Well, my place is with you. So I'm moving my home base here. That is, if you'll have me."

Clem blinked, unable to believe what she'd just heard. "But what about your job at the investment firm? You love that job. And what about all those people you said were counting on you?"

"I was getting burned out on that job. I think if I'd kept at it, it would have made me old before my time. And as far as the clients are concerned, there are plenty of bright young people lined up to take my place."

Clem, becoming more excited now, gripped his arms tightly. "Are you sure about this? Really sure? Because I don't want you to give up a career you love for me."

Will smiled warmly down at her. "I want you to know that my new career direction is something I'm really excited about. Before, all my clients were rich, old money people who were born with silver spoons in their mouths the size of Volvos. With my new newsletter, I'm going to reach out to people who never owned a share of stock in their lives. I'm going to teach them how to take a modest amount of money and make it grow so they can afford to send their kids to college and retire in comfort.

"I've been planning this project ever since you left Manhattan, and all my research indicates that it will be a great success. Regular working people need sound financial advice in language they can understand, and I'm going to give it to them."

"It sounds wonderful." Clem reveled in the fire in Will's eyes and the sincerity in his voice.

"And the best part is, I can publish this newsletter from anywhere, as long as I have a phone, a fax machine, and a computer. Of course, I'll have to make the occasional trip back to the city, so I'll keep my apartment. *Our* apartment. You wouldn't mind going back there with me as long as you didn't have to stay, would you? I mean, I think there were parts of the New York City experience you liked, unless I miss my guess." He gave her a wink and a hopeful, lopsided grin.

"Of course I liked it," she assured him. "I loved the restaurants, theaters, shopping . . ." Clem's mind reeled with the possibilities. Could it be that Will could live with her in the mountains and be happy? Would he tire of her, miss the stimulation of the city and his sophisticated friends? Would she ever be more than a novelty to him?

"But what about the people, your friends?" she asked. "I can't talk to you about global economies and all that worldly sort of stuff. . . ." She pushed herself away from him and took a few steps toward the stream, turning her back. "What if you get tired of me?"

Will followed her to the stream. He took her shoulders, more gently this time, and let his hands slide down to her waist. He pulled her back against his lean, hard torso but did not turn her to face him, as if afraid she might reject him again. Pressing his chin against her cheek, he said, "I fell in love with you the first moment I saw you. Since then I have loved you more and more each day. I cannot imagine spending my life with anyone but you. And I can't picture my life without you."

Will hugged her harder and whispered hoarsely, "This can work, Clem. I know it can."

Clem turned and looked up into his intense blue gaze. She loved him as she'd loved no other man, and finally she was convinced that he loved her, really loved her, for who she was. "You're right," she breathed. "I really think it can."

She could feel the tension leave his body as he turned her to face him. Wordlessly, he reached into his back pocket and held out a small velvet box. "I know you don't like me giving you expensive gifts, but in this case I hope you'll make an exception." He flipped open the box to reveal an exquisite, emerald-cut diamond solitaire ring. "Marry me, Clem," he said, his voice hoarse with emotion. "I love you."

"Yes. Oh yes." Clem flung her arms around his neck, and they held each other for a moment. All the happiness she thought she had lost came back to her. *Will Fletcher wanted her to be his wife.*

"Oh, and there's something else in this box."

Clem allowed Will to slip the ring on her finger. Then he removed the box's velvet base and revealed what was under it. It was the sapphire she'd found on the day they'd first met.

"I offered to give this back to you, if you'll recall, but you insisted I keep it. So I thought that maybe you'd cut and polish it and put it into my wedding band."

Tears spilled down Clem's cheeks. "I'll make you the most beautiful wedding band the world has ever seen," she vowed, looking up into his wonderful, dazzling blue eyes.

"I never doubted it for a moment."

They kissed for a long, long while, oblivious to the world outside their embrace, including the dog that stood at the bottom of the hill wagging her tail, wearing a red bandanna and what looked for all the world like a smile.

EPILOGUE

". . . And that," Clem concluded, "is the story of the beautiful bird and her brave Indian warrior." She set the baby bottle down on the porch beside her rocking chair, eased her three-month-old son onto her shoulder, and patted his back gently. As she rocked little Will, she looked out over the valley, appreciating the view she knew she would never tire of.

She'd spent most of the day working in her spacious home studio overlooking the stream while the baby played and napped on a pallet of quilts beside her. Will was due back at any time from a business trip to the city. His newsletter had been an instant success, and frequent trips to New York kept his financial contacts fresh. Although she usually accompanied him, she had stayed behind this time to make the most of a burst of creative energy.

On a typical day when Will was home, she worked or studied at her workbench while he conducted business at his computer setup across the room. They took turns tending the baby and followed any schedule they pleased, taking frequent breaks for hikes through the woods, coffee breaks on the front porch swing or—whatever they wanted to do.

She had just that afternoon met the design deadline for her new line of jewelry, and couldn't wait to celebrate with her husband. And that wasn't all they would celebrate tonight, she thought as she rocked her baby son.

Uncle Jess roared up on his scooter and let the engine sputter to a stop. He doffed the jaunty goggles he had picked up on his recent trip to New York City.

"You're looking pretty spry this morning," Clem observed. Jess climbed the steps with less effort than Clem had seen him use in years.

"Since Will set me up with that Manhattan rheumatologist, I feel like a new man." Jess settled into the rocking chair next to Clem's.

"Hmm. I was thinking that the spring in your step probably had to do with the attentions of a certain woman named Elaine." Jess blushed, a sight that Clem wasn't sure she'd ever seen before. "I must say, you clean up pretty good. It's been years since I've seen you in anything other than overalls."

"I'll tell you, having such a beautiful and sophisticated woman squire me around Manhattan was—well, it was something I never expected."

"If your arthritis keeps getting better, you'll be dancing up a storm on your next trip. Elaine is a former professional dancer, you know. She could really show you how to cut a rug."

Jess laughed. "I was a pretty fair dancer myself in my day, young lady. I just wish I got a chance to see Elaine more often."

Clem settled her baby onto her lap and gave her uncle a wink. "In that case, how would you like to go with us to New York next time we go? You can check in with your new doctor and go out on the town with the glamorous Elaine."

Jess smiled his gratitude. "Count me in. That's

some place Will has there on Central Park. The staff is great. That doorman is a real helpful fella. He'll do most anything for you if you ask him nice."

Clem raised an eyebrow. "I think it's safe to say that any friend of Will Fletcher's is a friend of the doorman's. I'm really glad that Will kept his apartment. Despite everything, I love to visit New York—the shopping, the culture, and nightlife. I'd just rather live here. Say, what's that package you have there?"

Jess set a small, gaily wrapped package on the floor between them and reached for his great-nephew. "Happy first wedding anniversary. I know Will's supposed to be back any time, but he knows how much you like presents. I'm sure he wouldn't care if you went ahead and opened it."

"I don't mind if I do." Clem handed her son over to his great-uncle, prompting the infant to gurgle and kick his feet vigorously. Jess made a funny face at the baby and received a squeal of amusement in return.

Clem tore away the wrapping, revealing a beautiful wood carving of her and Will's dream house, complete with the rockers on the front porch. She was delighted, not only by the gift, but because of what it indicated about Jess's condition. "You did this? Your arthritis really has improved. A year ago you couldn't have held a knife long enough to have carved anything, much less this masterpiece."

"That's right," Jess agreed, giving her a warm smile. "Thanks to you, Will, and the best specialists in New York, I think I can get back to making jewelry at the shop—that is, when I'm not babysitting for William Bartholomew Fletcher the fourth."

"You are the ideal babysitter, that's for sure. But I know you're happiest when you're working on your own jewelry designs." Clem rose and went over to give her uncle a big hug. "I can't tell you how happy I am for you."

Jess patted his niece on the back as she hugged him. "And I'm happy for you, too, girl. You've done pretty well for yourself over the past year. Not only do you have big Will and little Will, but thanks to the Internet program at the university you're on your way to a bachelor's degree in fine art. You'll be the first Harper to graduate from college." Balancing the baby on his knee with one hand, Jess wiped away a tear with his old bandanna. "Darned ragweed," he muttered.

"Thanks, Jess." Clem patted her uncle's balding head and looked out across the valley. "I can't believe how things have turned out, how incredibly blessed I am. I have the perfect man, the perfect baby, my dream house in the mountains, and my favorite uncle is healthier and happier than he's been in years."

"Not to mention an apartment on the Upper West Side of Manhattan," Jess said, winking.

"I have a feeling you're going to be using it more than Will and me, though. You'll probably turn it into your own private bachelor pad when you go up there to visit."

Jess made a face, and Clem laughed.

"Say, do you hear something?" he asked, squinting toward the place where the driveway disappeared around a bend. Clem gaped in surprise when she saw Will ride out of the forest on the back of a white horse.

"Here's your knight in shining armor now," Jess said with a chuckle.

Hardly able to believe her eyes, Clem bounded down the steps and across the lawn to meet him. "It's

him!" she shouted. "It's the hansom cab horse!"
Clem had never forgotten the horse she'd befriended
on her first trip to New York. She'd made a point of
visiting him on each subsequent trip since her mar-
riage to Will.

Will, dressed in jeans, boots, and a red polo shirt,
bent down and kissed Clem's forehead. "Happy anniversary, sweetheart."

"Do you mean it?" Clem stroked the horse's neck
and put her cheek against his silky nose, prompting
him to nicker softly with recognition and pleasure.
The horse, who'd always had a dignified but melancholy air, regarded his surroundings with keen interest. It was the first time Clem had ever seen him when
he wasn't wearing blinders.

Will laughed. "You can look this gift horse in the
mouth all you want. He's definitely yours. Of course,
I think he was yours in spirit from the first time he
met you."

"Where will we keep him?"

"In the stables, of course." Will gestured toward
the woods at the east side of the house. "I figured
we'd build them over there."

Clem stood on tiptoe to kiss her husband. "Thank
you! Thank you!"

Sensing a commotion, Ruby came bounding down
the mountainside, followed by three boisterous, half-
grown puppies. Wagging her bushy tail, the golden
retriever trotted fearlessly up to the horse, who lowered his head in curiosity and allowed the dog to sniff
his nose and, finally, lick his mouth. The puppies
scampered around the horse, who eyed each one
with eager interest and nuzzled the ones who dared
to venture close enough.

"I think they're going to be fast friends," Clem observed.

"Looks like they already are." Will reached down, put his arm around Clem's waist, and swung her effortlessly onto the horse in front of him, her full cotton skirt fanning out before her on the saddle blanket. They rode up to the porch, where Jess was playing peekaboo with the baby. "I left the horse trailer in the driveway of the old cabin. When we get back we'll make arrangements to board the horse with one of the farmers in the valley until the stables are finished."

Will nodded toward Jess. "Are you all set for babysitting duty?"

"Ready, willing, and able," Jess replied, turning the baby around on his lap so he could face his mom and dad. The old man held up baby Will's tiny hand and waved it. "Bye-bye."

"Where are we going?" Clem asked, leaning back against her husband.

"You and I are going on a camping trip to celebrate our first anniversary. You don't need to get anything together. I have the campsite all set up. If the baby needs us, Jess can call us on the cell phone, and thanks to Old Blue here we can be back in thirty minutes flat."

"We'll be fine." Jess waved them off. "Happy anniversary. See you tomorrow."

"Sounds like you've thought of everything," Clem said, squeezing Will's knee. "Let's get started. And by the way, 'Old Blue' is a dog's name, not a horse's name."

Will shrugged. "What do I know? I'm just a city boy."

Before they started off, they dismounted, kissed the

baby good-bye, and gave Jess some instructions about little Will's schedule. When they mounted up again and got onto the trail, the horse followed the path with confidence, as if he already knew the way to their destination.

"In all the excitement I nearly forgot to give you your anniversary present." Clem reached into the pocket of her skirt and produced a cheap, plastic snow globe with tiny model mountains inside and a sign that said, North Carolina is for Lovers. She shook it vigorously and the plastic snow swirled. Handing it to Will, she said, "For the man who has everything."

Will laughed delightedly. "How did you know that was what I wanted?"

"I know everything about you, except where you're taking me, that is. Where *are* we going exactly?"

Will settled Clem more closely against him. "Remember that stream where we camped next to the waterfall? I think that was when I first fell in love with you."

"Where you first saw me naked, you mean." Clem tilted her head back and looked into Will's eyes.

"That, too."

"So you finally admit it. You *did* see me naked that morning in the waterfall."

Will laughed. "I never said I didn't. I was just trying to be a gentleman, that's all."

"Trying to drive me crazy wondering about it, more likely. I suppose I should be glad you made an honest woman out of me."

"Oh, you were an honest woman before I ever met you," Will said, massaging her thigh with his free hand. "Not to mention beautiful, intelligent, charming, and talented, and loving. Speaking of loving, I thought since we're married now you might be persuaded to repeat the performance you put on that morning at the waterfall. I might even join you."

"Sounds like a good way to celebrate our first year together." Clem ran her hands up and down her husband's powerful thighs.

"This is only the first of many, my darling Clementine. The first of many." Will sighed with contentment and kissed his wife as they rode west, into the dazzling summer sunset.

BOOK YOUR PLACE ON OUR WEBSITE AND MAKE THE READING CONNECTION!

We've created a customized website just for our very special readers, where you can get the inside scoop on everything that's going on with Zebra, Pinnacle and Kensington books.

When you come online, you'll have the exciting opportunity to:

- View covers of upcoming books
- Read sample chapters
- Learn about our future publishing schedule (listed by publication month *and author*)
- Find out when your favorite authors will be visiting a city near you
- Search for and order backlist books from our online catalog
- Check out author bios and background information
- Send e-mail to your favorite authors
- Meet the Kensington staff online
- Join us in weekly chats with authors, readers and other guests
- Get writing guidelines
- AND MUCH MORE!

**Visit our website at
http://www.zebrabooks.com**

Coming October 1999 From Bouquet Romances